# Heart's Melody

## GRANITE COVE
### BOOK SEVEN

## DENISE CARBO

*For my sister-in-law, Rafaela. You're always the life of the party. Thanks for putting up with our crazy family.*

# Chapter One

Pain—it shapes who we are. Some moments in our lives mark us like inkblots on paper. From those points, our lives change and branch out in different directions and choices, like the root system of a tree. We can never be the same after those defining moments.

I kneel in front of the gravestone and brush off the debris at the base. Lichen has grown on the side. Next time I come, I'll bring a brush and clean it off. The cold from the ground seeps into me. According to the calendar, spring has arrived in Granite Cove. But Mother Nature hasn't quite let go of New Hampshire's winter. The foot of snow from the storm last week has mostly melted except for in the shadiest spots and the piles left behind by the snowplows.

The wind moans through the trees and lifts my hair, whipping it across my cheek and sending a shiver down my arms. A clump of hair snags on my glasses. As I untangle the mess and shove my hair back into my hood, a brown strand breaks off. My black parka is long enough to protect my knees from the damp ground, but the low heels I wore to work don't provide much protection for my chilled toes. Leaving school in my shoes instead of boots was a mistake, but I was tired and ready to go home. Granite Cove Elementary is in the throes of spring fever. My third graders are impatient for warmer weather even more than I am.

Being cooped up inside for months on end can turn even the mildest-mannered eight-year-old into something from a horror movie.

"Hi, Rosie." I briefly rest a hand on top of the carved angel perched above the headstone before stuffing both of them back into the pockets of my coat to keep warm. My gloves are still sitting in my desk drawer at school. I don't know where my mind was this after-noon. "You'll never guess what my students did today. You remember little blond, blue-eyed Zoe? She's usually sweet, quiet, and helpful, but today, she abruptly stood up from her desk and screamed at the top of her lungs for no apparent reason. When she finally stopped and I asked her why, she shrugged and said she needed to let her feel-ings out. She struck me speechless for a solid minute with that one." *Just one of the many times I've considered an eight-year-old might be smarter than me.* Then again, adults can't go around screaming in public places to let their feelings out. Kids frequently get away with things adults can't. Screaming alone in my house might be okay, though.

"Then this afternoon, Deacon, who admittedly isn't as saintly as his name might imply, decided to not only change all the names on the cubbies so the paperwork went into all the wrong students' sections but also somehow switched the contents of the backpacks of about a dozen of his classmates before I caught him. He winked at me and smiled as widely as you please, like I hadn't just caught him red-handed. He's going to grow up to be either a criminal or a politician. I'm not sure which." *Or both. He could definitely be both these days.*

A car inches past my gray wagon parked at the end of the row of headstones, and my fingers clench in my pockets. The driveways through the cemetery aren't wide enough for two lanes, and the only parking is outside the gates. In the winter months, there are usually fewer visitors, so parking my car there was less likely to impede anyone and prevent me from freezing walking back and forth. I wince as the hood of the passing car dips down, as they must have driven off the road to fit around my car. *It's too late to offer to move it now, right?*

The car rumbles past and continues through the graveyard toward the newer section. The smell of gas and exhaust trails in its wake. Sigh-ing, I glance up at the overcast sky visible through the branches of the oak tree towering over the half a dozen rows of gravesites lining this middle section.

"So, I have some news. You'll never guess who's getting married. Or maybe you already know. Sometimes I imagine you're watching us on a TV screen or something and snacking on popcorn. Brian proposed to Katy over the weekend. She said yes, of course. I knew he was planning on asking but not this weekend. I went ring shopping with him only last week and helped him brainstorm proposal ideas. But you know Brian. Impulsive is his middle name. They showed up for Sunday dinner and announced the engagement. Mom and Dad were over the moon."

I tuck my hair behind my ear and pull my hood closer to my cheek. "Katy said her parents are thrilled, and her mother is already talking about grandchildren. Can you believe it? They're not even married yet. I admit my eyes must've widened a bit when I started wondering if she was already pregnant, especially after she said they wanted the wedding this fall. I mean, what's the rush? But she wants to get married on her parents' anniversary and doesn't want to wait a whole other year for it. So of course, I got Brian alone later and asked him outright if Katy was pregnant. He rolled his eyes at me and said no. I still say it was a perfectly valid question." *My little brother, who was a confirmed bachelor less than a year ago, is suddenly not only engaged but also planning to marry in six months. Of course I'm going to ask a question or two.*

The same car comes back down the road and inches by my car. I wrinkle my nose as the same dirty-engine smells assault my nose.

"Anyway, so wedding planning is in full swing. I suggested talking to my friend Lucinda, who is a wedding planner, but apparently, Katy's mom nixed that idea. Brian says she's a bit of a control freak, and Katy struggles with standing up to her. Glad it's not me."

*Mostly glad anyway.* "I'm a little envious, watching all my friends and now my brother get married. Not that I'm not happy for all of them. I definitely am. It just seems like each of my friends is finding love, getting married, and starting families. I told you Tina and Kelly had their babies. I have a feeling Franny or Olivia will be next. Rebecca might surprise us, though. If I were a betting person—which we both know I am not—I would bet on Franny. She's got that look in her eyes every time she holds one of the babies." The book-club ladies are all finding love and starting families while I stand on the sidelines, watching.

Purple, yellow, and white crocuses bloom at my sides despite the snow and cold temperatures. Some leaves are brown and withered instead of green. Their lives are so short. "I should add some more bulbs, since they seem to be doing well here. I bet they'll spread and give you a nice carpet of flowers next year. What do you think? You always did like pretty things. The hyacinths and tulips I planted in the fall should be up in a few weeks. They're your favorite color, pink. I should've planted flowers instead of bringing them sooner. You'd have your very own garden by now if I had."

I huddle closer to the gravestone and duck my head against the wind. Rosie would like being surrounded by flowers. And as long as I don't plant anything too invasive or something that will spread everywhere, the cemetery manager said I can plant what I want. It seems rather apropos to plant miniature rosebushes on the sides of the headstone too. I glance up at the sun and the maple tree, which will cast partial shade over the area when its leaves come in. But it should be sunny enough for the bushes.

"Wedding planning should keep Mom and Dad happy for a good long while. At least through fall and the wedding." *And I hope give me a brief reprieve, if they're happy and preoccupied with Brian's nuptials.* "If she does get pregnant right away or within the next year, that'll extend their happiness, don't you think? Can you imagine them as grandparents? It's hard to say which way they'll go. They could be over-the-top involved, or maybe they'll be reserved and hesitant to get too attached." I shake my head. There's no reason to go down this obstacle-filled path just yet. Pregnancy and babies aren't the present. The wedding is. One major event at a time.

"I'm trying not to borrow trouble—really, I am. But I worry Mom won't be up to much wedding planning. Even with Katy's mom being controlling, some responsibilities will fall to the groom's family, right? I guess I'd better have Lucinda fill me in on all the details so I'm prepared. You know I'm a planner. I need to schedule whatever is coming so I can shift things around and make time for any tasks I need to take care of. At least I'll have more time over summer break." *I guess I'll have to put off that national park trip I've been planning for another year. I didn't have much hope I'd be able to get away anyway. Good thing I never actually worked up the courage to book anything.*

My shins and feet are turning numb from the cold, so I stand and brush off my legs. I touch my chilled fingers to the name engraved on the headstone—Rose Marie Lynn Frasier. Tears fill my eyes. "I miss you, Rosie. I really wish you were here. You always managed to cheer me up and make me laugh."

I rub my cold cheeks and force a smile onto my lips. "We have a birthday coming up. I'll bring you your favorite chocolate cupcake with pink frosting, as usual." *Maybe this year, Mom won't take to her bed for a couple of weeks.*

"Well, I'd better say goodbye before I turn into an icicle." I trace my fingers over Rosie's name and the words carved underneath. I pause over 'beloved daughter and sister' just as I do every time. *Will the ache ever ease?* My fingers drop, and I lower my head.

I stare at the dates on Rosie's headstone. I'll turn twenty-nine on our birthday. Our last party was for our ninth. I've had twenty years of lonesome birthdays.

"Good night, Rosie Posie."

The childish response echoes in my head. *Good night, Monie Lonie.* The image of us as two little girls giggling as we performed our nightly ritual from our twin beds side by side fills my head. We shared not only a room but a womb too.

*Chapter Two*

Brian's truck and an unfamiliar Jeep block my parents' garage. Frowning, I park behind the Jeep. I should've gotten details when Brian asked me to stop by after work, but I didn't have time because my lunch break was ending and I had to get back to class. I assumed it was wedding stuff, but that's not Katy's vehicle. She drives a BMW her parents passed down to her for her college graduation. I drum my fingers on the steering wheel. *Please don't let it be bad news.*

It's doubtful any answers will come to me while I'm sitting in my car in the driveway, so I grab my phone out of the holder attached to the car vent and open my door. The snow has melted, and my parents' lawn is that patchy brown and green before spring takes over and the blooming season is in full swing. I'll have to check with Bobby and make sure my parents are on his landscaping schedule this year. Otherwise, it'll likely fall to me to mow and take care of everything again. Maybe I can talk to Lucinda and Bobby at the same time and check two things off my list. They're always together these days anyway—engaged and inseparable. *What does it feel like to want to be with someone all the time?* I've always preferred having my own space and taking a break from people. It's hard to imagine letting someone encroach on my personal space or time, yet there's still this yearning inside me. Maybe humans are built that way to ensure the survival of the species. Either that or someone up there in charge likes the drama of watching people interact and make fools of themselves.

Voices reach me when I open the door and step inside. My parents' Cape Cod house isn't huge, and from the front door, I can partially see into almost all the rooms except for the den and bathroom. No one is visible in the living room or family room, but Dad gives me a wave from his chair at the pine kitchen table. Brian tilts his head around the corner. "'Bout time you got here."

I roll my eyes at him while I take off my shoes and coat. "School gets out at the same time every day, Brian. I told you when I'd be here."

Mom appears in the archway between the foyer and the kitchen. She clasps my hands and smiles. "How was your day? Oh, your hands are chilled. Would you like some tea to warm you? Why aren't you wearing gloves?"

I glance into the kitchen. My heart stumbles when my gaze locks on the man leaning against the end of the peninsula across from Brian. I blink a couple of times as my brain scrambles to process the scene—blond hair; tall, broad, muscular build; hazel eyes. And a dimple pops out as a smile spreads over his mouth.

*Succotash! Succotash! Succotash!* Brody Jackson stands in my parents' kitchen. This might be one of those times I wish I hadn't trained myself to substitute harmless words for swear words so I wouldn't inadvertently blurt one out in class. Succotash just doesn't carry the same punch. *Brody Jackon is back in Granite Cove.*

I guess I know who the Jeep belongs to. It's not exactly the Mercedes he used to drive or his parents' Porsche, which he crashed through the guardrails and into a pine tree when he was twenty.

"Hey, Mon."

His voice sends warmth through me. *Please don't let me blush.* He's the only one who ever shortened my name or gave me any kind of nickname.

I swallow hard. "Brody." I glance at my brother. *This can't possibly be why he wanted me to stop by, can it? Having his best friend show up in town after several years is an event for him, but what do I have to do with it?*

"Isn't it wonderful, Monica? Brody is staying at his parents' house this summer just like when you were kids." Mom walks by him and pats him on the arm. "I'll make you that tea."

"You sit, Mom. I'll make it." It will give me something to do while I figure out what's going on. I scoot past Brian and Brody, grab the teakettle off the stove, and fill it with water while I stare out the window. Our old swing set sits in the back corner of the yard. It's rusted and unsafe, but my mother refuses to let me have it removed. Visions of Brian and Brody playing on it as kids while I sat at the picnic table doing homework flash through my mind. I was the designated babysitter until they were in their teens and old enough to go without. *Although their teen years seemed to be when they needed the most supervision.* The two-year age difference between us felt more like ten. While I was getting all A's in school, helping out at home, and working at the library, Brian was barely passing classes and getting into one mischief or another with Brody.

After I set the kettle on the stove and turn it on, I take a deep breath, paste a smile on my face, and turn around. Brody is the only one watching me. Brian talks with my parents about his latest job, wiring houses in a new development. Working as an electrician for our uncle was a turning point for Brian. His plans to take over the business when Uncle Todd retires will help ensure not only his future but also any children he and Katy have. Brody left right around that time and stopped coming back during the summers. Maybe that had more to do with Brian growing up and not getting into trouble as much.

Brody walks over and leans his back against the sink next to me. "Brian tells me you're a teacher now."

"Yes, at the elementary school. And you? The last time Brian mentioned you, he said you were a musician."

"Yeah, it pays the bills," he says with a shrug.

"That's good." I can't imagine many people can make a living at music, so he must be decent to make enough to pay his bills. Then again, if he's spending the summer in his parents' house, maybe they're still supporting him. Brian told me when Brody dropped out of college that his parents had cut him off and kicked him out, but maybe they reconciled. "You're staying with your parents? How are they?" *Does this mean he's going to be around a lot?* It's not like Brian still lives here with Mom and Dad, so Brody will likely go to Brian's place, not here.

He stares at me for a moment before answering. "The same. They won't be here. Haven't been for years. It's usually rented out, but it needs some work. I decided to handle it since I need to be here for Brian's wedding." The corner of his mouth kicks up. "Surprised the hell out of me when he said he was getting hitched."

"Me, too, but he's happy and in love."

"What about you?"

I fold my arms and frown. "What about me?"

"You married? Engaged? Involved?"

*Nope. None of the above. Terminally single.* I'll probably be one of those old cat ladies, except without the cat. "No. You?" I hold my breath, waiting for his answer. It's hard to picture Brody married. He always had a line of girls after him but never one in particular.

"As single as ever." His dimple appears with his grin, and my stomach tumbles like I plummeted off a cliff. "Maybe you and I should make one of those pacts. If we're both still single at a certain age, we get hitched."

I gape at him for what feels like an eternity, but it's probably only a few seconds. "To each other?"

He shifts closer. "Is it really so hard to imagine?"

Heat spreads over my skin. *Have my parents turned up the heat in here?* No, it's not that hard to imagine. In fact, the thought crossed my mind one too many times right before he disappeared.

I drop my gaze over his navy-blue sweater and jeans, down to the blue socks covering his feet. The crush I developed on my brother's best friend was not one of my prouder or saner moments. *Does he know? Is that why he's talking like this? I thought I kept my feelings hidden, but why else would he be joking about something so ridiculous? Is he needling me about my former pathetic crush? Subtly letting me know he knows?*

I meet his gaze briefly before glancing away. No. He would've said something back then. He's just being his flirty self. He used to flirt with every female in his radius—except me. Which made sense. I was older and used to babysit him, for goodness' sake. Plus, I was his best friend's sister. And I was the complete opposite of his type. He dated the wealthy summer girls with their perfect faces and figures.

"Are you thinking about it, or have I lost you completely?"

*Lost me? Thinking about what? Did he ever have me? Want me?*

Brian walks over. "What are you two talking about over here?"

Brody shifts away from me. "Just catching up with your sister."

The teakettle sounds behind me, making me jump. "Anyone else want tea?" I turn and grab a couple of cups. Mom always says yes to tea. Everyone else declines, and Brian and Brody move to the table.

I practice my breathing exercises while I pour the water and get the tea bags. A few minutes back home, and Brody already has me wondering about things I have no business thinking about. He was only teasing and making small talk with his best friend's sister, probably just trying to break the ice, since I was obviously shocked to find him in my parents' kitchen.

Mom takes her cup from me with a smile and a nod. I slide onto the empty chair next to my dad and on the opposite side of the table from Brody.

"Now that you're both finally here together..." Brian grins and rubs his hands.

*What is my dear little brother cooking up now? What involves Brody and me together?*

"I want the two of you to be my best man and woman—both of you. You know, share the role. I couldn't pick one over the other. You're both my best friends."

*Brian wants me to be his best woman?* Tears threaten, and I purse my lips. "I'm so touched, Brian. Of course the answer is yes."

"That's double yes from me." Brody slaps Brian on the back and grins at me. "I guess the two of us have some planning to do, Monica."

My smile fades, and I swallow. Brody and I will have to work together on the wedding duties. My stomach flips over.

We're both adults. I've matured. I no longer let a crush derail my logical thinking or turn me into a tongue-tied idiot who blushes at the mere thought of him.

*This will be fine.* We can communicate by email.

"Give me your number, Monica."

I blink up at Brody standing next to me with his phone in his hand.

We can communicate by text. No reason to talk or meet in person.

*Everything will be fine.*

# Chapter Three

"I have some news to share before we discuss this month's book selection." Franny's hair glows like the flames in the fireplace she's sitting next to. Her lavender shirt stands out against the navy chairs and complements her red hair and ivory complexion. She's practically vibrating in her seat as her hands drum on her jeans-covered legs.

"Oh my god! You're pregnant!" Lucinda jumps up from the couch and rushes over to her sister. She moves so fast that her blond hair flows behind her.

"What? No, Luce, I'm not pregnant. Although I have started taking prenatal vitamins, and Mitch and I plan to try this summer."

Lucinda hugs Franny. "That's still exciting news. I can't wait to be an auntie!" She straightens her blue sweater as she returns to her seat on the couch next to Rebecca and Rachelle.

"We'll have another baby to spoil!" Kerry grabs my knee and grins at everyone in the room. Her hazel eyes practically sparkle.

I smile back before staring into the flames of the fireplace. The heat warms my skin, and the crackle of the logs soothes my nerves. She and I are part of the dwindling single-ladies group in the book club and in the school system we both teach in. I never thought I'd feel left out as my friends and coworkers found love and started families. It never bothered me before, but suddenly, I am feeling pangs of loneliness.

The excitement is contagious as everyone chatters about babies. Tina and Kelly both gave birth in the past year and exclaim over having babies to grow up together. I shove down a slight pang of envy. I'm truly thrilled for all my friends, but part of me wonders if it will ever be my turn. *I probably need to go on actual dates for that to happen.*

Rebecca clears her throat to get everyone's attention. "So, if it's not baby news, what is it?" She swings her foot back and forth over her crossed legs and spins her ring around her finger.

"Remember, ladies, we do need to keep the noise level down a bit since we do have guests staying upstairs." Rachelle points up.

I glance at the closed doors to the hallway. Three different sitting areas divide the ballroom, which Lucinda and Rachelle are calling the main room. When they hold a wedding or event here, they remove all the furniture and replace it with chairs and tables. Or in the case of holding the actual wedding in here like last month, they have rows of chairs and an arch for the bride and groom. They've turned the Granite Cove Inn from a neglected home into a sought-after wedding venue in less than a year. A lot of their success has to be attributed to Lucinda's skills and charm. Even the inn portion is thriving under Rachelle's management. Lucinda's friend Jackie manages all the finances remotely, but she's been visiting more often of late and has joined our monthly book-club meetings a few times. When they hosted the book-club ladies during their preopening stage, they gave us all questionnaires to fill out to let them know what was working and what they could improve. My only suggestion was to provide water bottles in the rooms so guests could take medication or relieve a dry throat without having to go downstairs. I couldn't think of a single improvement. It's not like I travel much, and the overnight stay was perfect from start to finish for me. I can still taste the sweet and tart lemonade Rachelle served and the blackberry tea with blueberry scones.

"Hear that, ladies? We're a rowdy bunch." Aunt Aggie slaps Sally on the arm. "Can you believe it?"

Sally snorts out a laugh. "Of you? Yes."

We all chuckle. My godmother has never been the shy or silent type.

Aunt Aggie keeps Uncle Dennis on his toes and often blushing. She's the complete opposite of my parents. *How did they ever become such close friends?* It gives credence to the opposites-attract phrase. Mom and Aggie have been friends since elementary school.

"Sorry, Franny. We got sidetracked. What's your news?" Lucinda gives everyone a silencing look.

Franny scoots to the end of her seat. "You know how Mitch has Bobby putting in those raised garden beds for me to plant vegetables this year?"

"Sure. Bobby showed me the layout he drew up. You're having an herb garden, too, right? And a shed?" Lucinda pulls out lip balm from her pocket and applies it to her lips.

"Yes, it's wonderful. He took my rambling dream list and is making it a reality." Franny waves a hand. "Anyway, when they were digging for the foundation of the garden shed, they uncovered a locked box."

Kerry gasps next to me. "You found treasure?"

Rebecca chuckles. "Leave it to you, Franny. You're living on the estate of your dreams with your famous, gorgeous husband, and now you find treasure?"

Franny clutches her necklace and smiles. "I am pretty lucky lately, but I'm not sure I would classify the contents as treasure just yet." She frowns. "Well, they might be to someone."

"Now I'm intrigued. What are the contents, and who would they be a treasure for?" I lean forward in my seat.

Franny takes a breath. "Mitch had to cut off the lock. It must have been down there for some time, because rust covered both the box and the lock. We were afraid whatever was inside would be ruined, but it was completely dry and intact. It only smelled a little musty."

"Get to the good part. What was in it?" Kerry rolls her hand in a hurry-up gesture and laughs.

"Patience is not your strong suit, is it? No wonder you teach at the high school instead of the elementary school." I bump her shoulder in jest.

"One of many reasons, but yes. I'm one of those who skips ahead in a story to find out what happens."

I gasp. "But doesn't that spoil the story for you?"

Kerry shakes her head. "Not at all. Now be quiet so we can hear what was inside."

I mimic zipping my mouth closed and turn back to Franny.

"A journal."

"Whose?" Tina snatches a cookie off the tray and eats it while staring at Franny.

"That's the thing. We have no idea. None of the names I've read match the previous owners or occupants of the house."

"Did you read it?" Rachelle frowns and sips her wine. "I mean, it's someone's personal thoughts that they not only locked up but also buried. Sounds like they wanted it kept private."

Rebecca rolls her eyes. "If they wanted to ensure no one ever read it, then they should've burned it, not hidden it for someone to find."

Franny nibbles on her lip. "See, that's been my dilemma. I didn't want to invade someone's privacy, but on the other hand, I'm really curious. That's why I wanted to ask what you all think."

"Then let's take a vote. Everyone who agrees Franny should read it, raise your hands." I scan the room as everyone's hands shoot up except Rachelle's and mine.

Franny widens her eyes. "You don't think I should read it, Monica?"

"I'm on the fence. I understand Rachelle's argument but also agree with Rebecca. But there's something else to consider as well. You might find something out about someone that may be unsavory or even illegal. That could lead to even more questions and consequences."

"Yes, I found that out before with Mrs. Roberts." Franny looks at Lucinda.

"That was a shock, especially for Bobby, but I don't think he regrets knowing." Lucinda shrugs. "I believe it's always better to have the knowledge, then you can decide what to do with it."

*Would I regret knowing my parents' secrets?* I guess it would depend on the secrets. It's hard to realize your parents are only people too. They make mistakes like everyone else. Of course, Bobby's parents made more than most—especially his mother. If the woman can even be called a mother. Child abandonment was probably one of her lesser crimes. I'm sure Bobby wishes she never came back into his life. But then again, if she hadn't, he might have never known the truth about his father's accident or the type of person the woman who spawned him is.

"Well, it's my vote that Franny brings the journal to the next book club, and we can all read it and figure out who it belongs to." Rebecca folds her arms and leans back on the couch.

"You think we can? I mean, figure out who it belongs to?" Franny stands and takes a cookie from the plate.

"Of course. Look at us." Rebecca gestures to everyone in the room. "We're a group of intelligent and successful women. We kick ass."

I chuckle. "My research skills are fairly top-notch. It could be fun solving the mystery together."

Kerry tilts her head toward me. "So you're on board with reading the journal?"

"Yes, as long as everyone acknowledges the possibility that we might not like what we find out. People keep secrets for a reason, after all. And they're not always pleasant." Everyone has secrets. I certainly have my own. Aunt Aggie is the only one in this room who knows about Rosie, and I intend to keep it that way. People look at you differently when they know you've suffered such a loss. Book club is my haven. My past doesn't define me here.

Aunt Aggie snorts. "It could also be boring as dirt."

Rebecca raises her glass. "There is that possibility." She turns to her sister. "What about you, Rach? Do you want to abstain from reading the journal?"

Rachelle wrinkles her nose. "No. My curiosity is piqued too."

Lucinda claps. "We have a mystery to solve."

# Chapter Four

The peony cage lists to the side, and the rungs slip apart for the dozenth time, so I wrestle them back together and push the legs into the dirt. The smell of damp earth rises from the ground. With my gloved hands raised, I step back warily, waiting for the infernal contraption to defy me yet again and spring apart. The peony poked through the soil only a few days ago, but past years have taught me they will grow fast. Erecting the cages over the peonies once they are already grown is even more difficult. I spent way too many hours putting the cages together around the delicate giant blooms the past couple of years, so I promised myself this year, I would put them up at the first hint of growth. If the space in my garage weren't so precious, I'd tape them together and put them away fully constructed instead of collapsing them every fall.

My backyard isn't huge, but my little ranch house sits on a couple of acres that are all mine. The cedar tree in the middle of my yard sealed the deal for me when I toured the house. The rich, evergreen scent brings me back to my childhood, when Rosie and I played hide-and-seek at my grandparents' house. I always hid in their cedar closet, and Rosie always found me.

Wiping my perspiring brow with the back of my wrist, I walk back into my garage through the side door and press the button to open the front. The mechanism clanks as the door slowly rises on the track. My spring-cleaning list extends as I stare at the dirt, dust, and cobwebs on the windows and ceiling. The smell of exhaust and what I'm guessing is oil taints the air and makes me wrinkle my nose. Leaving the door open for a while should allow fresh air to replace the stale air in the garage. I hoist an Adirondack chair from the pile of outdoor furniture in the corner. The solid-wood chair isn't too heavy, but it is unwieldy. My walk across the yard and around the house to the back-yard makes me look like a cross between a crab and a sumo wrestler. I place the red chair under the apple tree, which isn't showing any signs of life yet, and glance at the trio of birdhouses in an array of bright colors hanging from the branches. Fairly soon, I'll be able to sit here, listen to and watch the birds, smell and see flowers, and relax with a cup of coffee or tea—or maybe a tall glass of lemonade or iced tea once the sun chases all the lingering cool temperatures out of New Hampshire.

"Are you a fan of the cold, or are you being hopeful and trying to spur on the warmer weather by putting out lawn furniture?"

I whip around and have to grab the chair before I fall headfirst over the roots peeking out of the ground.

Brody walks toward me with a wide smile on his too handsome face.

*What is he doing here? And why now of all times when I'm covered in dirt and probably stink from exertion?* I pat my hair, hoping it's not sticking up all over the place, then realize I'm still wearing gloves and probably smeared dirt all over my hair. *Wonderful.*

He stops a few feet in front of me. "So which is it?"

I stare at him blankly while I try to figure out what he's talking about. *Right. Weather.* "Hopeful, I guess, because I'm not a fan of the cold. What are you doing here?" *And how do you know where I live? And why didn't you call and give me fair warning so I could be more presentable? Like maybe dressed in clothes that aren't stained or bagging on me because they're a few sizes too big.* I glance down at the sweatshirt I'm wearing. It is, in fact, several sizes too big because it's Brian's.

*Oh god, did I even brush my teeth this morning? Of course I did, right? I always do right after my coffee. But did I have coffee this morning?*

Brody chuckles and waves a hand in front of my face. "Hello? You okay, Mon?"

"What?" I blink at him and realize he must've been talking while I had my mini mental breakdown.

"I told you I'm here so we can catch up and discuss our best-man duties. Or best person."

*We couldn't do that over the phone?* "Um, well, I'm not exactly prepared for that conversation. Why don't we set a time next week? We can chat on the phone."

Brody frowns briefly before shrugging. "Why talk on the phone when we can talk in person? I'm not a big fan of talking on the phone. Besides, I can help you while we talk." He turns and jerks his thumb in the direction of my garage. "Didn't I spot another red chair still in the garage? I'll bring it over."

"No, you don't have to do that."

He ignores me and keeps walking as I stare at his back, which is covered in a black jacket. My gaze drops to the jeans covering his lower half and lingers on the way his muscular thighs make quick work of the distance.

"No trouble. Be right back."

I squeeze my eyes shut and sigh. *Should I chase after him? For what?* Brody always did what he wanted, no matter what anyone said. At least this will give me a few minutes to recover and plan how I'm either going to get rid of him or at the very least get inside and clean up.

"Where do you want it?"

I pop my eyes open. Brody carries the red chair effortlessly, like it's a small toy. I dart my gaze down to the ground and point at a spot close to the other chair.

He places it at an angle beside the other one. It's exactly how I would've placed it myself.

"Thanks."

"No problem. You want the table and chairs and the grill on the deck?"

I open my mouth to decline but pause. It would be an enormous help. I usually have to wait for Brian to find time to help me because the table and grill are beyond my capabilities. "If you don't mind..."

"Not a bit." He saunters back to the garage. It takes me a bit to follow him because I'm too busy ogling his ass. Mentally slapping myself upside the head, I practically jog to the garage.

He hauls the grill while I carry a chair. He stacks three chairs together and walks out of the garage. I glance at the two remaining chairs. *Should I stack them together?*

Images of me tripping and breaking a bone or pulling or tearing a muscle flash through my mind. No, I know my strengths, and muscle power isn't one of them. I pick up one chair and carry it around the side of the garage and onto the deck. Brody passes me on the way and returns with the last chair and the umbrella before I even set the chair down.

"Up to helping me with the table?"

"Of course." I trot after him.

We grab opposite sides of the table and trudge around to the deck. "You got plans tonight?"

I wobble my side of the table. *Plans? He's not asking me out on a date, is he?* No, of course not. That would be ridiculous. He's asking because he wants to talk about wedding duties. "Nope. No plans. You?" *Why can't I be one of those people who effortlessly lie?* I could make up a date—even a boyfriend. My only plan is to sit at home and catch up on the latest episodes of my favorite shows.

"Yup. I plan on grabbing a pizza from Joe's. Care to join?"

"Oh."

We arrange the chairs around the table.

Brody stops. "Don't break my heart and tell me Joe's Pizzeria is no longer around. It's a Granite Cove staple, and I've been salivating thinking about their pizza."

"No, Joe's is still there."

"Great. Meatball and onion still your favorite?"

*He remembers my favorite pizza?* "Uh, yeah, it is."

"So it's a date, then. Five o'clock good? I'll pick you up."

*A date? Brody Jackson is asking me on a date?* So many sensations rush through my system that I'm suddenly lightheaded. I grip the top of the metal chair and stare at the deck beneath my feet. I really shouldn't have skipped breakfast this morning. My brain doesn't seem to be working properly. My brain's processing speed is sluggish. I guess I must've skipped coffee this morning. I cringe. That also might mean I forgot to brush my teeth. *Ugh.*

Brody can't be asking me out on a date. He means *date* as in two people meeting at a designated spot, not romantic in any way. No man would hit on me the way I look right now, least of all summer playboy of Granite Cove, Brody Jackson.

*Oh no, is this one of his pranks? Does adult Brody still pull those? Why not?* His partner in crime, Brian, my devilish little brother, still does. That must be what this is!

"Have I lost you again, Mon? Where do you keep going?"

He's not smirking or anything. But then again, he and Brian fooled me on more than one occasion.

"So help me, Brody Jackson, if you're planning to play some awful prank on me, I promise you I'll have my revenge, and it'll be soul crushing... for you."

He raises both hands in the air like I'm holding him at gunpoint. "Hell, Monica, I learned my lesson a long time ago when you stole all my clothes at the lake and left me freezing in the water. I couldn't get out for hours unless I wanted to be arrested for indecent exposure. There were two families playing on the beach. Parts of me were so shriveled I worried there was permanent damage." He places a hand over his heart. "I solemnly swear never to pull a prank on you again."

My lips twitch. "That was pretty epic. But you totally deserved it. You ruined my date with Andy. He never spoke to me again after you and Brian scared the hell out of him and made him think a spirit or demon possessed his car. He believed I was in on your prank." I stalked Brody for two weeks, waiting until he decided to go skinny-dipping in the lake to cool off. I knew it was only a matter of time. Both Brian and Brody had gone skinny-dipping on numerous occasions. I just had to be patient until Brody was alone.

Brody grins. "He was so scared he pissed his pants." He rubs a hand over his mouth. "That was one of our better ones. It took us weeks to figure out how to program his car to play music, honk, and have the lights turn on and off." He chuckles and sobers when he glances at my face and sees I'm not sharing in his laughter. "He was a prick, anyway, and wasn't good enough for you."

I might have to give him that one, since Andy had developed a reputation as a cheater and rumor spreader. He'd spread one about me being a terrible lay despite that we'd never even kissed, and I was still a virgin at sixteen.

"It's a miracle I ever dated at all in high school, thanks to you two. Remember that bucket of water with orange food dye you rigged to dump over my head? I missed my first dance because of you and Brian."

Brody winces. "Brian was grounded for weeks for that one."

I study his face. Brody hadn't been grounded. He probably wasn't even punished. His parents didn't seem to have much interest in being parents. Brody spent most of the summer at our house. Not having his best friend to hang out with was probably a punishment for him too.

"I can't say I'm too remorseful over that one, since it was my first wet-T-shirt experience, and I crushed hard on you all summer."

My vision blurs as I stare at him. *He had a crush on me?* Granted, he was only twelve at the time, since I was fourteen. *But still, Brody had a crush on me?*

"You look so shocked. Come on, Mon. Surely you had to know I had a major crush on you? I followed you around all summer."

"Yeah, pulling more pranks."

"Don't you know that's how a boy shows his affection to the girl he likes?"

I teach third graders. Of course I know that. But my fourteen-year-old self certainly never saw it that way. And he got over any crush he may have had long before I developed my own crush on him.

I glance at my watch—three thirty. "If we're going to grab a pizza tonight to discuss wedding duties, I need to get washed up. Why don't I meet you at Joe's?" That will make it feel less like an actual date and keep my imagination in check. Although I know my mind is going to fixate on Brody having had a crush on me.

# Chapter Five

It's a Saturday evening, and Joe's is as busy as usual. All the green booths lining the walls of the square Federal-style building are full. Luckily, I snagged the last table for two. Unluckily, it's by the kitchen, and everyone picking up a takeout order walks by me to the counter. I've already seen two of my students and three parents of my former students. One of the perks and downsides of living in a small town—the odds of running into someone you know is high.

A whoosh of cold air envelops me as the door opens again. It's not Brody. I glance at my watch. It's only four fifty, so there's still time. I'm always early—one of my virtues or flaws, depending on the way you look at it. At least I wore jeans instead of the long work skirt I briefly contemplated wearing. I don't want Brody thinking I consider this in any way an actual date.

Maria stops at my table to see if I want a refill of my diet soda. I've been sipping it for the past ten minutes as I try not to look like I'm waiting for someone, which is exactly what I'm doing, and I even had to tell Maria when she wanted to take my order. I smile and nod as I hand her the glass. The frayed edge of the plastic menu tickles my wrist as I rest my hands on the table.

*What if he doesn't show?* It wouldn't be the first time a guy stood me up. *What if his vow not to play any more pranks was a sham? What if his declaration of a crush was a lie too?* It makes more sense for it to be a lie. I have never been a girl boys had a crush on. I was the one boys talked to when they wanted my help to go out with one of my friends, the one all my friends felt totally secure with leaving their boyfriends with at parties or dances. They would never dream one of their boyfriends would be interested in me. Because they never were. I was the buddy—the third or fifth wheel.

Cold air whips around me again when the door opens. Brody walks in, and his gaze latches on to mine. He grins, and I smile back as a wave of relief washes over me. He showed.

He stops at the chair across from me and scans the restaurant. "This place is packed."

The door opens again, and he glances over his shoulder then frowns back at me. "You must be freezing sitting here."

I shrug. "The heat from the kitchen helps a little."

"You want to get out of here? We can get the pizza to go."

"Oh, if you want to. We could take it back to my house." Less scrutiny, and thank god I had the foresight to clean up a bit before I left.

He smiles. "I'll put in the order." He walks up to the counter, and Maria shoots across the restaurant to beat any of the other waitresses waiting on him. Maria is a flirt and has been since high school.

I deliberately turn away, not wanting to look jealous, even though our relationship is completely platonic. But I feel a small pang of envy as I hear her sultry laughter. I glance at the window and the glass door, hoping for enough of a reflection to see what's going on. *Is Brody flirting back?* It's too fuzzy to tell.

"All set. We have half an hour. You want to take a drive?"

"Sure." I grab my purse. "Let me pay for my soda."

"It's taken care of." He steps behind my chair and pulls it out.

I awkwardly stand, clutching my purse, while he holds my coat out for me. It's not a date, but he's already being more gallant than any of my recent dates.

Brody places his hand on my lower back as we walk out of the restaurant, then he points at his Jeep in the parking lot. "I'm over there."

He opens the passenger door and waits while I get in. *A gentleman?*

*When was the last time a man opened a door for me? Other than a relative?* He starts the engine and turns up the heat. "Where do you want to go?"

I shrug. "I've lived here all my life, Brody. You're the one who's been gone a long time. Where do you want to go? Any of your old hangouts you want to check out?"

"Not really. I drove through town when I first got here, and I've been to Hanson's, picking up groceries."

"What about friends other than Brian?"

He shakes his head. "Brian was my only real friend."

"That can't be true. You were always surrounded by people." Girls chased him for obvious reasons, but the guys hung around him too.

"You can be in a room full of people and still be alone. Same applies. None of them were anyone I trusted or called a friend."

I've certainly felt alone in a room full of people before. I give Brody a sideways glance. He's not the Brody I thought I knew. We're both adults now. People grow up and change. But maybe I never really knew him as well as I thought I did. "I'm perfectly happy sitting right here if you are."

His dimple pops out as he grins. "No place I'd rather be."

*That damn dimple.* It made my heart flop over for the first time when I was eighteen and he was only sixteen. He and Brian saturated me with the hose when they corralled me involuntarily into their water fight. I slipped in the mud from all the water, and Brody wrapped an arm around my waist and saved me from falling. I remained upright, but my heart nose-dived into a two-year long crush before he left Granite Cove and never returned. He kept in touch with Brian over the years, but as far as I knew, he never returned to town.

"Is this your first time back in Granite Cove?"

"No. I came back a few years ago for a couple of days. Saw Brian."

"Oh, I don't think he mentioned it." That wasn't surprising. Brian tends to forget everything as soon as someone tells him.

"He said you were practically engaged to some guy." Brody watches a couple walk into Joe's. "I figured you'd be married by now."

"I was never engaged." I scrunch my nose. The only person Brian could be referring to is Aaron. We were together for five years. "I don't know why Brian would say I was engaged or close to it. Aaron and I never discussed marriage." We never discussed anything about the future, really. We were both too comfortable to break it off when we should have and let the relationship go on way past its expiration date.

"Why didn't it work out?"

I shrug and look out the window. "Nothing major. We wanted different things. We were more friends than anything. He's married now with a baby on the way." He moved on and married the first woman he dated after me within six months. I guess he knew what he wanted when he found it. And it definitely wasn't me.

"His loss."

I smile at him. "What about you? Any close calls? Great loves?"

His gaze wanders over my face. "No." He taps his fingers on the steering wheel. "Which is why you should consider that marriage pact I mentioned the other day."

I snort out a laugh and look out the window at the restaurant as a family of six shuffles through the door. "Sure. What age do you want to pick? Fifty? Sixty?"

"How about thirty?"

I whip my head around. "Very funny. I'll be thirty next year." My twenty-ninth birthday went pretty much the same as it has been for the past twenty years—a family visit to the cemetery with Dad supporting Mom while she sobs; Brian making an excuse to skip dinner; Mom taking to her bed. At least this time, it was only for a couple of days. My thirtieth will probably be more of the same. "Are we going to get married then or wait until you turn thirty? If we go by my age, we'll have to start planning now."

"Sure. Where would you like to get married? Here in Granite Cove or somewhere exotic?"

I roll my eyes and lean my head against the seat. *I can play this game. Why not?* It's a lot more fun than what my actual birthday will be like. "Somewhere exotic. On a beach with palm trees. Although that might be because the warmer weather is overdue, and I can't wait for summer."

"I can get behind that. How about Bali?"

"Okay, you make all the arrangements. We can do it on my thirtieth birthday. Do you want to tell my parents and Brian, or should I?"

He grimaces. "That might be our first snag. Brian warned me away from you a long time ago. We were teenagers then, so I'm sure it's not a big deal anymore. Maybe."

I laugh. "Sure he did. And I'm also sure you're afraid of my little brother."

"Not kidding, Mon. He noticed my gaze on you once when we were all out on the boat. Shoved me overboard into the lake and said no, not ever."

His voice holds no amusement. I shift in my seat. Warmth spreads through me at the thought of Brody admiring me. "I remember that day. We were on your parents' boat. I thought the two of you were horsing around like always." One minute, Brody and Brian were behind me while I reclined on the bow, and the next, I heard a splash, and Brody was in the water. They laughed together later on and hadn't seemed to be arguing. *Could Brian really have warned Brody off? Why?*

I shake my head. It doesn't matter. We're just joking around anyway. It's not like we're really making a pact or getting married. "Like you said, we were teenagers. Besides, we need to get serious and discuss Brian's wedding and our roles."

"Sure. Bachelor party. Strippers, right?"

"Over your dead body."

# Chapter Six

The scent of butter and sugar drift from the bakery section of Hanson's grocery store. They don't compare to Franny's creations at the Sweet Spot, though. Her bakery is on my reward list after I get my mother home and help her put away all her groceries. My mouth waters at the thought of a piece of cheesecake from Franny's. I scan the list I made for Mom and Dad and cross off the lettuce I just put in the cart. Mom peers at the tomatoes and leans closer to sniff the ones still connected to their vines. I smile slightly. She's done that since I was a kid. Every time I smell tomatoes on the vine, I remember Dad's vegetable garden and Mom teasing him since it was ninety percent tomatoes. They haven't had a garden in years. The plot still sits in their backyard, waiting. It's covered in weeds, and the surrounding fence needs to be repaired, but it's another reminder of when life seemed to stop for them—all of us in some ways.

"Pick out tomatoes, Mom. They're on my list."

She hesitates over a few different packages as I scan the list again. These trips to the grocery store seem to get longer every time. It's good to get her out of the house, so I can't complain if she wants to linger.

"I was thinking you and Dad might enjoy some seafood. They usually have a nice selection of salmon. What do you think? You want to splurge this week?" When she doesn't answer, I look up from my list. She stands frozen in front of the display with a package of tomatoes in her hand. I step closer. *Please don't let her have one of her episodes now.* "Mom?" *What if she goes catatonic on me in the store?* It's like she disappears from her body completely when she does that. My heart pounds in my ears so loudly that I can barely hear the person on the loudspeaker telling someone to go to aisle ten.

Her face is completely drained of color, and the hand holding the tomatoes shakes. I take the package and squeeze her ice-cold hand. "Mom?" I follow her fixed gaze and suck in a harsh breath. A jolt of recognition shudders through me. Nancy Swift.

The woman's features are seared into my brain—small blue eyes; oversize nose; large ears she covers with her dyed-blond hair with dark roots. I'll never forget her. Despite the years, I could pick her out of a crowded room, let alone a sparsely populated produce section.

*Why now? Why here?*

She laughs, and the woman standing next to her turns around. *Holly?* It must be. She's older, my age. Of course she is. She didn't freeze in time. She grew up. *Why do I still picture her as a little girl?*

I shake my head and drop the package of tomatoes into the cart. I have to get my mother out of here before we're spotted or she loses it completely, so I slip my arm around her waist and gently steer her away. "Mom, let's go look for that salmon, okay?"

"Penelope."

I swing back. Nancy Swift stands three feet away with her daughter, Holly, staring beside her. When my mother doesn't respond, her gaze switches to me. The perplexed frown on her face clears, and a hesitant smile spreads over her lips. "Monica?"

"Mrs. Swift. Holly." *How am I going to extricate us from this nightmare?* Perspiration dampens my spine and pretty much every other surface of my body as my mind spins to latch on to an exit strategy with the least damage.

"How are you?" Her gaze flits between Mom and me.

That's certainly the question of the century. *Would shouting, 'How the hell do you think we are?' be too attention gathering?* "Fine. You?" It's a lie but a necessary one. My arm tightens around my mother's waist as she sags against my side. I straighten my spine and plant my feet to bear the added weight.

"We just had my bridal fitting." Holly waves her hand, showing a modest-size engagement ring.

"I needed a few things from the store, so we popped in." Nancy gives me a forced smile.

A lead weight drops in my stomach. "Congratulations." I suppose I could say that Brian is getting married as well, but that would only prolong the conversation and torture.

Mom trembles in my arms.

"Please excuse us. My mother isn't feeling well." I practically drag Mom through the store, leaving the cart with all the groceries behind. I can feel the Swifts' gazes on our backs. Or maybe it's just my imagination.

"Almost there, Mom. Just a little farther." Sweat pours off me as I search for my keys with one hand and support my mother with the other. I hit the unlock button and let out a breath of relief when the locks click open. "Here we go." I open the door and help my mother into her seat, fasten her seat belt around her, and shut the door. The light floral scent of her perfume envelops me.

Once I get to the back of my car, I lean against the cool metal and catch my breath. When I unzip my coat, the chilly air soothes my overheated body. I glance up at the blue sky. It's probably the only time I'll be thankful for the warmer temperatures not to have arrived.

*What are the odds?* They must have gone to Kelly's store for her wedding dress. Dress to Impress is the only bridal store in Granite Cove. *Why couldn't they go somewhere else?* Surely there must be another store that sells bridal gowns closer to them. Not that I begrudge Kelly any business, but she *is* married to a famous actor. Holden Fox is rich. She doesn't need the income. I squeeze my eyes shut and take a deep, cleansing breath. I need to get out of here before they come out of the store, and I need to get my mother back into a calm frame of mind.

She doesn't look at me as I slide into the driver's seat and fasten my seat belt. She stares at her hands clutched together in her lap. I start the car, turn up the heat, and once warm air flows, direct the vents toward Mom.

The trip out of town passes in a blur, and I drive on automatic while my mind spins. *What if this sets Mom back? Should I call her therapist? Dad?*

"I didn't recognize Holly."

My mom's whisper startles me. She's staring out the window. *Progress? What should I say? Change the subject or encourage her to talk? Dammit.* I should've become a psychologist instead of a teacher. Maybe then I'd know the right thing to do.

"I pictured her as the same little girl with blond pigtails and freckles. The freckles are gone." She glances at me. "Did you see any freckles?"

*Freckles? She wants to talk about freckles?*

"No, but she might've covered them with makeup." If Mom wants to talk about freckles, then we'll talk about them. At least she's conscious and talking.

"Oh. I didn't think of that."

She's not retreating. She's actually talking coherently about people who have to be extremely triggering for her. Mom never talks about the incident or anyone involved. No one does. We all skirt around it like it's a snake in the grass.

"Nancy hasn't aged much." She turns to me. "Have I?" She looks back out the window. "I feel like I've aged a century."

Mom has lines by her eyes and mouth. She hasn't been to a salon since she had a panic attack and I had to pick her up. Now Dad trims the ends of her hair a couple of times a year. Nancy Swift probably visits the salon every few weeks and has a bathroom full of beauty products. I didn't notice any lines or wrinkles, but I was hardly looking for them. She probably has injections and surgery to keep her appearing young. I never thought Mom cared about looks, but she must if she noticed how Nancy Swift looked. I squeeze her hand. "You're beautiful, Mom."

She doesn't acknowledge my words. "My angel was beautiful."

My gut clenches. *Is she going to talk about Rosie?* She never does. She just cries if someone inadvertently mentions anything to do with her. I hold my breath and wait. *Could this be a breakthrough she needs? Who would have thought seeing people involved in Rosie's death could help her in any way?*

Guilt oozes from my thoughts. I wanted to punch them both. It wasn't cathartic in the least for me. God, and if Paul had been there, too, I might've strangled him with my bare hands. Holly will walk down the aisle with her father on her arm, while my sister will never have the chance.

"Rosie would've made a beautiful bride."

The picture swims in my head—Rosie all grown up, blond, beautiful, and in a wedding gown. Tears threaten. "Yes, Mom, she would have."

"My angel was so special. She would've done wonderful things."

I swipe at my wet cheek as I pull into her driveway. Dad's car is parked in front of the garage. Good. He's home. She won't be alone, and I can go home and wallow in my misery.

Except I'll have to explain to Dad what happened. I wonder how he'll handle it. He might make an excuse and leave, then I'll have to stay. I wince at the selfish thought as I park the car.

Mom's face falls. "We left the groceries."

"I know. I'll have to pick them up later for you."

She walks up to the house with me beside her. Dad opens the front door with a smile. It disappears as his gaze darts between us, but he says nothing. He helps Mom with her coat.

"I think I'll make some tea." Mom wanders down the hall, into the kitchen.

Dad waits for the sound of water filling the kettle. "What happened?"

"Um, we were at Hanson's, getting groceries." I eye my father's face while I tap my fingertips together. "Nancy and Holly Swift were there. They came over and said hello."

His jaw clenches, and his gaze narrows.

"She was upset, but I got her out of the store, and she seemed better —even talked a little about Rosie."

Dad's bottom lip trembles, and he stiffens.

I swallow hard and wait for his response. *Will he avoid any talk of her? Or will Mom's broaching of the subject be enough to prompt him to do the same?*

"I'm going to go check on your mother." He puts his hand on my shoulder. "You should head on home." He kisses me on the forehead and walks down the hallway.

I lean against the front door and stare at the ceiling for a moment. *Will it be this way for the rest of our lives?* It can't be healthy for any of us. I straighten and call out, "Goodbye, Mom."

"Bye, honey." Her voice is low, but she is in the kitchen. She sounds good, not spiraling.

The door closes behind me, and I hesitate on the steps while staring at the green door. It's been the same color for decades and is marked up and dull in places, but like a lot of things about this house, it doesn't change.

I walk to my car, get in, and close the door. *Am I a terrible daughter for leaving? Should I go back inside?* I drop my head on the steering wheel. *What would Rosie do?* She would probably have found a way to make them laugh. Rosie could always make people laugh when she was around. She liked to entertain people. While I avoided the attention, Rosie shone and exalted in it. We were twins but so different, not just in looks but in personalities too.

Rosie would probably have performed on a stage somewhere or in front of a camera.

*If it were me instead of her, would my parents still be the fun, smiling parents I remember from before? Would Rosie have kept them happy?*

The question has popped into my head often over the years. The answer too. Rosie was joy personified. She would've found a way to make them happy again.

I reverse out of the driveway and turn the car toward home. I'm no longer in the mood for the Sweet Spot—nor have I earned the reward.

## Chapter Seven

The patterns of light on my ceiling slowly disappear as the late-afternoon sun lowers in the sky. Nestling farther into the corner of my couch, I pull my knees up to my chest. I thought coming home, putting on my comfiest pajamas, and pouring a glass of wine would help ease the stress of the day, but instead, all I can do is play back the event in my mind over and over again, looking for flaws and missteps. As soon as Mom spotted the Swifts, I should've gotten her out of the store. No, I should've been paying closer attention to my surroundings instead of staring at the grocery list and counting the minutes until I could finish Mom and Dad's list and get her home and head to the bakery for a treat then alone time. If I had seen them first, the entire episode could've been avoided, and I wouldn't have seen the sadness and disappointment on Dad's face or be sitting here wondering if Mom is even now spiraling back into depression.

The fruity taste of the wine coats my tongue as I take another sip. My soft flannel top soothes my skin as I rub the hem between my fingertips. *Why didn't my parents pick up and move away? Why stay and be faced with reminders day in and day out?* Surely a fresh start might have helped us all forget and move on—better than we have anyway. The only one who seems to have coped is Brian, but then again, he was only seven when Rosie died.

If we'd moved, the chances of our running into the Swifts or anyone from the past would be practically nonexistent. The Swifts hadn't even lived in Granite Cove but two towns away, and they still moved after the accident. *Were they running away from the guilt? Had they even felt any?* An accident by definition rules out culpability. Holly was just a child, so she could hardly be blamed, and Nancy wasn't there, but Paul, he was there. He was driving. He may not have caused the deer to run into the road, but he could've reacted better and not driven into a tree. *How could his daughter walk away with a few bumps and bruises while Rosie, who sat a couple of feet away from her, never woke up?* I don't wish Holly had taken Rosie's place. I've never wished that. *But why did it happen?* I've asked that question too many times to count.

It took a few years for teachers and neighbors to stop looking at me with pity and whispering behind my back. Some adults seem to think children can't hear or understand when they act that way. I was nine, not two.

The doorbell rings. *Who could be at my door? I didn't forget any plans, did I?* No, I only planned to come home and relax tonight. I glance down at my flannel pajamas then at the door. *What are the odds whoever it is will just go away if I don't answer?*

A blurred head appears in the frosted side panel of the door. I freeze. *Can they see me? Who is it?* It's a man. *Brian? Did he hear about the incident from Mom or Dad?*

A knock sounds on the door. "I know you're in there, Monica. Open up."

*Why is Brody at my door?* I grimace and gaze down at my pajamas. They cover more than a lot of people wear in public these days. Heck, teenagers prance around in pajamas in public all the time. I can't be judged for sitting in my own home in my pajamas.

He knocks again.

I sigh and place my glass of wine on the coffee table. He's not the type to go away. I wouldn't put it past him to try all the windows and doors. If he climbs behind the bushes in front of the window five feet to his left, he'll see me as clear as day.

The dead bolt clicks, and I open the door a few inches. "Now isn't a good time, Brody."

His hazel eyes scan me from head to toe. "What's wrong?"

"Who says anything is wrong? It's just not a good time."

He tilts his head. "You're in your pj's at…" He glances at his smartwatch. "Five o'clock. Monica Frasier does not put on nightclothes in the daytime. I clearly remember you lecturing Brian when we were around fifteen about how the sun was shining, so he needed to get dressed in clothes and not lounge around in his pajamas all day even if he had no intention of going outside."

He's right. I lectured Brian more than once about getting dressed when we were kids. "People change, and maybe you don't know me as well as you seem to think you do."

"Your eyes are red from crying."

I purse my lips and look away as the tears threaten once again.

"What's wrong, Mon?"

*When did he start calling me Mon? Sometime in our late teens? Why does it make me feel special to him when he calls me that? It's just a nickname.*

Brody gently pushes open the door. He glances around inside, and his gaze rests on my half-full wineglass on the table. "Got any more of that wine?"

I wave at the bottle sitting on the counter separating my living room from the kitchen.

He saunters over while I shut the door and crawl back into my corner of the couch and pull the blanket off the back of the couch to wrap around me. Brody returns with the bottle and another glass. He tops off my glass and sits right next to me. I glance around at the empty chairs and the other half of the couch he could've chosen to sit on then at him. "What are you doing here, Brody?"

"I thought we could grab a bite to eat and do some planning. We didn't actually get around to it the other day."

No, we didn't. We chatted about a dozen or so other topics instead, mostly the past and the mishaps he and Brian got into.

He puts his hand on my knee. "Tell me what's bothering you."

I stare at the back of his hand. His skin is tanner than mine. If we put our hands side by side, his would probably be twice the size of mine. The warmth of his hand seeps through the blanket and my pajama pants. Mine are always cold. I glance away. *What should I tell him? How much does he know?* I'm sure Brian must've mentioned Rosie at some point growing up. We don't talk about her to each other often. I don't talk about her to anyone. It's too hard. The therapists my parents sent me to when I was a kid were useless. They asked endless questions and nodded and said, "That's interesting," to anything I actually responded to. *How was any of that supposed to help?*

"Did Brian ever tell you we had a sister?"

"Yes, he mentioned her a few times over the years."

"What did he say?" Brian rarely talks about Rosie to me and never to my parents. *What would he have said to his friend?*

"He told me she died in a car accident."

"What else? You said he mentioned her a few times."

His fingers flex against my knee. "He brought her up when he felt you or your parents were being unreasonable or overprotective. He thought they acted that way because of losing her."

That makes sense. My parents were very protective. Neither of us was ever allowed to ride with anyone else in a car. We weren't able to get our driver's licenses until we were eighteen and only then because we were legally adults. I guess I was protective of him, too, once I started babysitting him and taking on more and more of the responsibilities. Of course he would've lashed out and complained to his best friend about the restrictions.

Brody takes my hand and holds it resting on my knee. "Is this about your sister?"

I rub my hands on my thighs. "I took Mom grocery shopping, and we ran into the Swifts. Two of them anyway. Holly and her mother. Rosie was in the car with Holly and her father, Paul. Rosie was the only one seriously injured—the only one who didn't make it. Mom was understandably upset."

"What about you? It obviously upset you too." He rubs his thumb over my palm.

"It was a shock, but I was more worried... am more worried about how it will affect Mom."

"You're afraid it will cause her to have another breakdown and have to be institutionalized again?"

"You know about that?"

He hesitates as he stares at my face. "Brian told me it's happened a couple of times."

"Three, actually. It's been several years, though. The last one was when I was in college." I was sitting in my dorm room, studying, when Aunt Aggie called me. It was the first time I was living away from home, even though it was my junior year. I had to commute for my first two years to help take care of Brian and home. But once Brian graduated from high school, I thought it would be okay. It wasn't. I moved back home after less than a semester.

"So you're worried this will set her back. How upset was she?"

"Actually, she handled it better than I thought she would. She even talked to me on the way home. Mom brought up Rosie, which she never does."

"She might be strong enough to handle it now."

"Maybe."

"How did you handle it? Seeing them."

"It pissed me off." I glance at him and away. "Probably shouldn't say that."

"Why not?"

"Because I should be past all that after twenty years. It was an accident, and of course they went on living their lives. Holly is getting married. She showed us her wedding ring. She and Nancy were at a bridal dress fitting. It's why they were in Granite Cove."

"They don't live in town?"

I shake my head. "They never have. We went to gymnastics together. That's how we knew them."

"I didn't know you did gymnastics."

"I stopped after Rosie died." *I stopped a lot of things.*

"You have a right to be angry. I don't think there's a time limit on grief."

"Have you ever lost someone?"

"My grandparents. They were more like my parents than my own ever were. It was their house on the lake that we spent the summers in.

The one I'm staying at now. They died within a few months of each other a few years ago. My other set of grandparents died when I was a kid."

"I'm sorry. I didn't know."

"I never talked about it much. I was too busy being angry at the world. Showing my parents I was the screwup they always claimed I was."

I squeeze his hand. "You weren't a screwup. You were definitely wild, and you made me worry, but you were always a good friend to Brian. And now here you are, showing up for him when he's about to get married and letting his sister cry on your shoulder. You're a good man, Brody. More than I ever gave you credit for, and I'm sorry for that."

His mouth quirks in a small smile. "You're hardly crying on my shoulder, but you're welcome to anytime you like. Now, how about I order takeout and we polish off this bottle of wine while we wait for them to deliver the food. They do deliver all the way out here, right?"

I chuckle. "They do, actually. I've never gotten it, but my neighbor does."

"Good." Brody scrolls on his phone. "What are you in the mood for?"

"Surprise me. I'm not that picky."

He peeks up from his phone. "Mexican? I've got a craving for enchiladas."

"Sure. There's a new restaurant in town I haven't gotten around to trying, but I can't remember the name of it."

He scrolls for a few seconds. "Tequila Sunrise?" He glances up. "We can get delivery from them." He turns his phone to me. "Take a look at the menu."

"Just order me a rice bowl or something."

He studies me. "Okay, but no complaining if you don't like what I order."

I raise my hand. "I promise."

Brody gets up and paces my living room while he places the order. *Who would've thought he would be the one to comfort me and make me feel better?* I guess I didn't give him enough credit when we were teenagers. Sure, I had a crush on him, but that was because he was hot—still is. Actually, he might be even handsomer now.

Blinking, I look away. I definitely don't want those thoughts popping into my head. I will not get another crush on Brody Jackson.

He plops down next to me and hands me my glass of wine. "All set. Now, why don't you tell me a happy memory about your sister, and I'll tell you one of mine about my grandparents? It helps make the grieving bearable when we focus on good memories instead of the loss."

I smile. "When did you get so wise?"

"I wouldn't go that far, but I've made enough mistakes to know what doesn't work."

"You mean sitting by yourself in your pajamas, drinking wine and ruminating over everything you should've done differently doesn't help?"

He chuckles. "Nothing wrong with the pajamas or the wine. It's the alone part and beating yourself up about things you can't change." He taps the bottom of my glass and lifts it toward my mouth. "Drinking with friends and remembering the good things is highly recommended."

"We're friends now?"

He stares at me. "Aren't we?"

I take a sip of my wine. "I suppose we are."

His lips kiss my cheek, and I almost spit out my wine.

"Good answer. Now finish your glass of wine, because I ordered margaritas to go with our meal."

My cheek tingles from his kiss. I force the wine down my throat and pray I don't choke. It was an innocent, platonic kiss. My brain knows this. My body, however, seems to believe differently.

I take a subtle deep breath while hiding my face behind my glass of wine. It really has been too long since I've been romantically involved with anyone if a simple kiss on the cheek sends me into a tailspin. I need to go on a date.

# Chapter Eight

*Lucinda: Emergency meeting tonight at Rebecca's*

My gaze darts between the text message and the road. *Emergency meeting? What constitutes an emergency in book club?* I frown at my phone. *It was in the book-club text group, right?* I glance out the windshield, the rearview mirror, and both side mirrors. The rain is coming down so hard it sounds like sizzling bacon as it hits my car. My wipers can barely keep up.

Nope, I'm not going to give in to temptation and check while I'm driving. I'm less than twenty-minutes away from home. Even if there were no cars around and I was driving on my rural road instead of through town, I wouldn't cross that line. My parents couldn't survive another loss. Or god forbid I hurt someone else because I couldn't resist checking a text.

A series of beeps signaling new texts come from my phone as I drive through town. I have to peer through my windshield to see the traffic lights. I need to upgrade my car to read my incoming texts to me. *How ridiculous is that thought? Trade in a perfectly good car just so I'll have one with the ability to distract me while driving and read out texts.*

Once the center of town is in my rearview mirror, I flip on my signal and turn into the parking lot of a professional plaza with an insurance agency, a Realtor, and an odd assortment of businesses. I may still be less than ten minutes from home, but my curiosity and worry will drive me nuts if I don't check. I park and remove my phone from the holder.

Yup, it is the book-club text group. And there's been a string of texts since the first.

*Franny: You're going to scare everyone! No one panic. It's not an emergency.*

*Rebecca: I don't think emergency is the correct word. It's more of an impromptu meeting to discuss our little mystery. Btw check your emails, ladies. I scanned the journal and sent everyone copies.*

*Lucinda: Apologies! Excitement got the best of me!*

*Olivia: Ooh! Franny and I have already started it, and I'm already obsessed!*

*Franny: Thankfully, I haven't burned anything and Olivia hasn't crashed the bakery's website she's updating.*

*Olivia: Actually, I'm scheduling social media posts, not updating the website, but the fear is real.*

*Barbara: I'm in!*

*Lucinda: Are you two standing in the same room texting?*

*Franny: Maybe.*

*Olivia: Don't judge!*

*Lucinda: No judgment. I'm jealous! I haven't read it yet.*

*Rebecca: Not too many customers came in looking for flowers today, so I binge read it.*

*Franny: You're done already?*

*Olivia: No spoilers!*

*Rebecca: I couldn't help myself, and my lips are sealed.*

I chuckle as I read through the texts. Franny says Sally can't make it. Sally still hasn't mastered texting, so Franny or Aunt Aggie usually keep her informed, depending on whether Sally is working at the bakery that day or home. Rachelle says she won't be able to make it because the inn is full. Kelly is in Texas, so she won't be there either. Tina chimes in that she can't make it either, but she'll start reading tonight.

*Kerry: I'll be there but a little late.*

I had planned to stop by my parents' to check in. Even though I took them their groceries yesterday and they both seemed fine, I can't help worrying the shoe is going to drop at any moment. I nibble on my lip. It's always fun to get together with the book-club ladies, and I'm curious about the journal and what they want to discuss during the meeting. Before I can change my mind, I shoot off a reply.

*Monica: I'm in.*

After clipping my phone back in the holder, I drive out of the parking lot. I should have just enough time to change, grab something to eat, and make a quick phone call to check in with my parents.

*What do I have to wear tonight?* I skipped laundry day over the weekend because of the encounter with the Swifts. Then I couldn't bring myself to do it during the week because I have cheaper electrical rates on the weekends, which is why I do my laundry then. I puff out a breath. I have a drawer full of comfy leggings I can always wear. It's not like the ladies will mind.

My phone lights up as I pull into my driveway. A GIF of baby polar bears climbing all over their mother plays. *Aw, so cute!* I grin as I park my car. Brody has taken to sending me these random GIFs since he stopped by over the weekend. I do a quick search and send him one of a pony and a dog playing together. I used to think Brody and I were as different as that pony and dog, but maybe I was wrong, or we've just both matured.

* * *

A chorus of greetings meets me as Ian ushers me into his house. "And that's my cue to leave." Ian chuckles and kisses Rebecca on the lips. "Love you, babe."

"Love you too. Have fun with your brothers."

He looks back at the room full of women. "I'd say don't do anything I wouldn't do, but I doubt you'd listen." He points at all of us. "Behave and don't burn my house down."

Rebecca rolls her eyes as we all laugh. "Like you and your brothers aren't the ones more likely to burn anything down. We, unlike you hooligans, are respectable, responsible businesswomen." She kisses her brother Drew on the cheek as she helps him put on his jacket. "And you'd better not corrupt my brother."

After scrubbing his sister's kiss off his cheek, Drew grins from ear to ear like he really hopes Ian and his brothers will do some corrupting tonight.

"I make no promises." Ian winks and leaves with Drew.

Rebecca shakes her head as she locks the door behind them then turns and smiles. "Now, who wants to try the Moscow mule recipe I found? It's made with raspberry vodka, and it's delicious. I went out and bought these adorable copper mugs to serve them in."

Hands shoot into the air, including mine. I walk past the pool table and into the living room. I've admired the open floor plan and cathedral ceiling on previous visits. I love my cozy house, but this dramatic design suits both Rebecca and Ian.

Barbara leans against the kitchen island, which is longer than the width of my entire kitchen, watching Rebecca prepare the drinks. "Did Ian teach you how to make these? It must be handy having a pub owner for a husband."

"He most certainly did not. I helped Rachelle come up with a new marketing offer for the inn. She was trying out a taste testing offer, so we researched various popular drinks, and I came across this one. Ian's pub offers the standard Moscow mule, which is good, but this is scrumptious." She hands the first mug to Barbara. "What do you think?"

Barbara takes a tentative sip, and her eyes widen. "It's good. I was afraid it would be sweet, but it's not. There's only a hint of the raspberry." She takes another sip. "I like it."

Rebecca hands out more mugs as we all enter the kitchen.

Lucinda pushes herself onto the counter and crosses her legs as she sips her drink. "So, we called this meeting to discuss strategy and assign roles to discover who wrote the journal."

Franny jumps up next to her sister and pops a handful of nuts into her mouth from the array of appetizers on the island. "I'm only a third of the way through it, but full warning, it's a tearjerker. Olivia and I went through an entire box of tissues today."

Olivia sits on one of the stools at the counter separating the kitchen from the living room. "I won't spoil it for anyone, but it's not all sad. There are some happy and funny parts too." She turns to Rebecca. "You've read the whole journal. What would you say the tone is?"

Rebecca tilts her head and purses her lips. "Without giving too much away, I'd say I don't think anyone will be disappointed. The woman writing the journal has a sense of humor, but she's also shockingly honest about her feelings and faults. She doesn't edit out the less-than-complimentary parts."

I sip my drink, which is a tad stronger than I anticipated. This will be my only one of the evening, since I have to drive home. "My curiosity is piqued. I only had a chance to open the email before I came over, but it surprised me. The journal is more contemporary than I thought it would be. I assumed it was written at least several decades ago."

Lucinda points her manicured nail in my direction. "Me too. I was expecting to read about hoop skirts or something. But I think the woman is more like our parents' age." She glances around the room, then her gaze rests on Rebecca. "Is that right?"

"There are a few references throughout the book that make me believe you're accurate. Maybe slightly older."

Franny and Olivia both nod.

"What are these tasks you mentioned assigning?" Barbara picks a shrimp off the plate and takes a bite.

Rebecca picks up her iPad. "In order to find out who wrote the journal and why they buried it on Franny and Mitch's estate, we need to put our sleuthing caps on."

"Should we really track them down? I mean, they buried it for a reason." If I wrote a journal full of my deepest thoughts then hid it, I don't think I'd want strangers confronting me over it. Besides, if it's as personal as Rebecca implied, then it would be incredibly awkward to face this woman if she's still alive and confess we read her journal.

"Trust me—when you read the whole journal, you'll want to know the answers."

Lucinda raises her hand. "I'm a research guru, so I'll head to the library and see what I can dig up."

"Good. I plan to go to the town hall and research records." Rebecca swipes across her screen and taps something.

"What about the museum? They might have some information. I went with the boys on a scout trip a few years ago and was amazed at all the town history compiled there."

"That's a great idea, Olivia." Rebecca taps on her screen.

"I can stop in at the local paper. They have to have back issues."

Rebecca points at me. "Yes."

Barbara munches on a piece of celery. "What about me? What should I do?

The doorbell rings, and Rebecca goes to answer it. She calls over her shoulder, "How about internet duty? We'll need a couple of people seeing what they can find online."

"I can do that." Barbara picks up another piece of celery and swipes it through the dip.

Kerry comes inside, smiling. "Hey, everyone. Sorry I'm late."

We catch her up to speed as she takes off her coat, gets a drink, and samples the appetizers. "I'm a whiz at finding stuff online, so I'll sign up with Barbara for that."

"Perfect. And once everyone has read the journal, we should meet, and we'll probably have some more ideas to discuss." Rebecca puts down her iPad. "I also added the police station to the list to see what information is open to the public. If one of the ladies not here wants to tackle that or maybe one of us can when we finish our task."

We all stare at Rebecca. *Police station? Is there a crime mentioned in the journal?*

She mimics zipping her lips. "Read the journal."

# Chapter Nine

The doorbell ringing is followed by a hard knock on my front door. I groan and pull the blankets over my head. It's the last Sunday morning of the month and my one morning to sleep in and not worry about having to be somewhere, doing something for someone.

The knocking is followed by what suspiciously sounds like a dog barking. I flip the blankets off my head and squint at my bedroom door like I can somehow develop laser vision to see who is knocking on my front door with a dog and why. Nope, no laser vision, and I'm still half blind, so all I see is a blurry mess resembling my bedroom door and the painting of Neuschwanstein Castle in Germany on the wall next to it. The castle is on my bucket list. Well, it would be if I actually had a bucket list. Something else for the imaginary bucket list—make an actual bucket list. A girl's gotta have dreams.

They might go away and believe I'm not home, unless they already spotted my car in the drive. I still haven't finished my garage-cleaning spree, and there's still no room for my car. *Who do I know who owns a dog and might knock on my door?* No one comes to mind. A sound that resembles a dog whine or a broken kazoo comes next.

*What if the person is knocking on my door because they hit a dog in the road and need my phone to call a vet?* The guilt strikes hard and fast. I can't lie here if there's an injured animal on my doorstep. My conscience definitely cannot handle that.

I swing my hand at my nightstand and grope around until I feel the familiar metal frames of my glasses and slide them over my eyes. My world comes into focus as I climb out of bed just as the doorbell rings again. I trip over my slippers by the bed and stumble out into the hall, promptly stubbing my toe on the doorframe.

*Dammit!* I need at least ten minutes to become a functioning adult when I wake up.

Wincing, I limp my way to the front door and wrench it open—belatedly realizing I should've looked first in case it's an ax murder or someone luring me to open the door by thinking there's a hurt animal.

Nope, it's not an ax murderer but Brody with a small dog sitting next to him on my front porch. The dog tilts his head, his large ears flop over, and he raises his small paw to me. *Adorable.*

I blink at him then at Brody. "Why are you standing on my steps with a dog at..." I raise my wrist and glance down to see the time. I forgot to put my watch on. Okay, I may need twenty or thirty minutes to fully wake up in the morning, which is the reason why I always set my alarm an hour earlier than I need to so I have plenty of time for coffee and waking up.

I glance back up at the way-too-handsome-for-his-own-good man standing on my steps at whatever time in the morning it is. His dimple winks at me as he grins. At least, that's how my sluggish brain interprets the facial movement.

"Sorry. It's nine o'clock. Thought you'd be up. I wouldn't bother you if it weren't important." His gaze scans over me, and his grin gets wider.

Every muscle in my body locks in place as my brain finally wakes up. *Please tell me I'm wearing clothes and didn't decide to sleep naked last night. Please. Please. Please.*

I can't force my eyes to look down. If I do, then I'll have to face the reality that I might've opened the door with nothing but my birthday suit on and Brody can see every extra pound, stretch mark, and weirdly shaped mole on my body. No wonder the dog looked at me funny. He's probably wondering who the crazy lady is that his owner brought him to. *Wait. When did Brody even get a dog? Wouldn't I have known about this already?*

My hand twitches at my side and brushes against material. *Okay, I'm not completely naked. Is underwear much better, though? Yes, anything is better.* The material is soft but loose, so not underwear. Images bombard my brain of me getting dressed in shorts and a tank top before crashing in bed last night.

I almost sag against the door in relief. I'm wearing clothes. Only skimpy shorts and a tank top without a bra, but at least I'm not naked. *Who would've thought there would be a situation in which I'm actually thankful to be standing in front of my former crush in nothing but shorts and a tank top?*

The brown-and-black dog tilts his head again, and I swear he's grinning at me like he knows exactly what I'm thinking.

"When did you get a dog?"

"He's a recent addition. His name is Hank."

I shift my gaze from the dog to Brody. "Hank?"

He shrugs. "Came with the name."

"Hmm." *How do I extricate myself from this situation? Would it be rude to slam the door in his face and run back to my room and pretend none of this happened? Probably.* Besides, Brody won't let me get away with that. He'll probably follow me inside. And if I lock the door, he'll come knock on my window. He's done it before. It may have been more than a decade ago, but he doesn't give up. He and Brian asked me for a ride and if I said no, they pestered me until I gave in. I locked the door to my room, and Brody showed up at my window while Brian continued to wheedle through my door. Brody bribed me with the promise of a peanut-butter-and-fudge sundae. *Wish he had one now.*

I glance at him then the dog again. He's never going to let me live this down. It'll probably be brought up at family functions for years. *Remember that time Mon answered the door in skimpy shorts and top?*

"You...um..." He points at my face and frowns.

*Oh lord, what's on my face? Dried drool? That bag of chocolates I tried to drown my emotions in last night?*

His thumb rubs down my cheek. "Think it's just a mark from sleeping on a sheet or blanket too long."

*Wonderful.* I have sleep face. It probably looks like the creases of a road map.

I sigh heavily. "What are you doing here, Brody?"

He tucks his hands into his pockets, and his grin turns sheepish. "I need a favor."

If he needs a favor, then I might be able to negotiate with him into forgetting this morning ever happened. It's not like he took a picture and shared it all over social media, which is exactly what my brother has done and would do. Depending on the favor, of course. He's standing on my porch, so he doesn't need me to bail him out of jail. I look at his Jeep parked behind my car. There's not enough room in there to hide a body, so he probably doesn't need my help to cover up a murder. So his favor can't be too bad.

I wrap my arms around my waist as the cool morning temperature registers in my brain, and gooseflesh sprouts over my skin, and my nipples decide to say hello. *Don't look down, and stop squirming. You'll call attention to them.* I lock my arms and knees in place.

Brody's gaze drops and lingers.

My nipples preen under the attention, and I turn and dash into the house. I leave the front door open behind me but slam my bedroom door as I yank one of my brother's oversized sweatshirts over my head and hobble around the room as I pull on a pair of jeans.

This is what I should've done as soon as I realized I wasn't dressed. No. This is what I should've done before I ever answered the door. Now Brody will think I still have a crush on him—if he ever knew about the first time, which I'm really hoping he didn't.

I hang my head and count to ten silently. *You are an intelligent, accomplished woman. You are not a nerdy, overweight teenager crushing on your brother's best friend anymore.*

This could be much worse. I could've answered the door naked. I didn't. There is a silver lining. He could believe my reaction was solely due to the chill in the air. It's not like that time at the lake when I stood there in my bathing suit with my mouth open, practically drooling over Brody walking out of the lake, and I was picturing myself drying him off with my hands and possibly tongue—only to have my fantasy interrupted by a group of teenage girls pointing and staring at me, laughing. I was never sure if they were ridiculing me for my reaction to Brody or for my generous body stuffed into a modest one-piece bathing suit. I didn't wait around long enough to find out.

I'll make him believe it—with confidence and by completely ignoring the situation and acting like it never happened.

Yes, that is my plan. It's a sound plan. I nod, straighten my shoulders, and as nonchalantly as I can, waltz out of my bedroom with my head held high.

Brody is standing in front of the closed front door with Hank once again sitting at his side. His dog is well-behaved. If I thought about what kind of dog he might have, I'd probably envision a pedigreed dog, not the undetermined breeds Hank seems to comprise. I also think it would be more of a destructive tornado racing around the house than the calm, disciplined dog sitting next to his owner.

"He's house-trained. I promise."

"Good to know." Good. He's not going to mention my mad dash inside for clothes or anything else prior to it.

He smiles and rubs his hands together. "Hank has all his training. He doesn't pull on a leash, doesn't bark and go crazy at the sight of a squirrel, doesn't chew on anything, and he makes an excellent watchdog too."

I give both him and his dog an absent smile.

*Wait. Why is he listing all of Hank's admirable qualities?*

I glance between him and the dog. *No.* He's not going to ask me to dog sit his dog.

"It would just be for a few days. I have to go out of town. I have all his food, dog bed, leash, and toys in the Jeep." He jerks his thumb behind him.

I shake my head. "I don't do pets."

"Are you allergic?" Brody frowns. "Brian had a dog, Foolish. That goofball dog was a riot."

He did, and he was named appropriately. "I'm not allergic." At least I'm not going to sneeze, break out in hives, or stop breathing anyway. It's more of a mental allergy.

"You don't like dogs?" He stares at me like I've just announced I'm a convicted felon.

"Of course I like dogs. Who doesn't? I just don't take care of them."

Brody glances around my living room. I know what he sees. I like things neat and organized.

"He won't mess anything up, and if he does, I'll replace it. You're my only option, Mon."

*How can I be his only option?* I'm sure there are dozens of women ready to dog sit for him as soon as he crooks his finger at them. Of course, I'm not sure I would trust any of the women he dates to take care of a living creature.

*What about Brian?* Surely his best friend would be a better option. Brian loves dogs. He was completely brokenhearted when Foolish passed away a couple of years ago.

His gaze narrows slightly, and he says, as if he can read my mind, "Brian is too busy with work and Katy. Besides, I think Katy *is* allergic."

Hank does that head-tilt thing again in which his ear flops over half his face. I know now where the term *puppy-dog eyes* come from because it's like the dog is pleading with me.

Brody widens his eyes and gives me the adult-male version, and it's like my heart does have strings he can pluck.

"How many days is a few?"

Brody grins, and Hank woofs. *Did they practice that?*

"Four. Five at most. I'll get his stuff." Brody is out the door before I have time to point out I haven't actually agreed yet.

He returns with a dog bed tucked under his arm, a bag overflowing with pet paraphernalia, and a giant bag of dog food.

I look at the dog food then the dog. That could probably feed him for at least a month. *It better not be a month.*

Brody kisses my cheek, pats Hank on top of the head, and slips out the door.

The warmth of his kiss and the heady feeling of his skin brushing mine momentarily addles my brain.

*Is he getting more stuff? How much does one small dog need?*

His Jeep rumbles to life. *He's leaving?* I look at Hank still sitting in front of the door. He wags his tail, walks right past his dog bed, and leaps onto the couch.

"Why do I suddenly feel like I've just been played?"

# Chapter Ten

"Oh my god!" I drop the journal in my lap and wipe the tears off my face with the bottom of my shirt. *Sixteen, pregnant, and feeling like her life is over. What would I have done?* I roll over and grab a tissue from the box on my nightstand to blow my nose.

I didn't have sex until I was in college, so it wasn't something I ever had to seriously contemplate. There were a couple of teenage pregnancies while I was in high school, and since there were less than one hundred kids per grade, that was more than two percent. Technically, if you only counted the girls, then it was even higher. They weren't close friends of mine, so I wasn't privy to their feelings on the subject, but they didn't act like they were contemplating suicide over being pregnant. But they both dropped out of high school. And one of them still lives in town with a few more kids, still married to her high school sweetheart. So it didn't work out so badly for her. I had one of her younger kids in my class when I first started teaching. She seems pretty happy. So I guess she's a success story. Meanwhile, I'm still single with no prospects of ever getting married or having children.

Still, it's not the same situation. Linny isn't pregnant by her high school sweetheart. She's pregnant by an older guy who calls her Linny Baby. Ick factor right there. *What does she see in him?* I get that when you're sixteen an older guy can seem mature and sexy. She said he made her feel desirable and special, even though she knew it was wrong.

I slide my hand over the journal. Linny is so honest about her feelings, especially since she's so young. If I ever wrote in a journal, I don't know if I'd be as forthcoming or enlightened about my faults and mistakes. I'd probably only write in it when I was upset and angry at the world, highlighting everyone else's faults rather than mine. But I suppose that would be significantly telling on its own.

I still have still two-thirds of the journal left to read, so I know she doesn't commit suicide—at least not yet.

As depressed and angry as I got growing up, I never contemplated suicide. I could never do that to my family. They already lost one child. I couldn't put them through that again—even when I felt they would've preferred I'd died instead of Rosie.

*Not going down that path tonight.*

The lump under my blankets at my feet moves. Hank hasn't used his dog bed once in the two days he's been here and apparently likes sleeping under the covers as if he were a person. He stares at me until I give in and lift the covers so he can crawl inside. It's like he's using some sort of dog telepathy on me or something. Either that or I'm just a pushover. Yeah, that might be the one.

Linny had plenty of opportunities to date guys her age. She was apparently a guy magnet. Even her steady boyfriend, who was in college and, from her words, worshipped the ground she walked on, wasn't enough for her to resist William. He's not Will or Bill and certainly not Willy or Billy. He sounds like a pretentious jerk who creeps on teenage girls. *Why would she cheat on her boyfriend for him?* I don't understand it.

If I had a guy who was head over heels in love with me, I'd thank my lucky stars and do everything in my power to make the relationship work.

*Would I, though? Or would I wonder if it was all an act or if he had ulterior motives?* It's hard to say, since I never had a guy who loved me. Even Aaron, who I dated for almost five years, never told me he loved me. I never told him either. We were friends first in college and sort of fell into a relationship. There was no grand passion.

My first boyfriend in high school only asked me out because my friend turned him down. He cheated on me and broke up with me within a month. The second guy I dated couldn't really be called my boyfriend. The nicest thing he ever said to me was "I don't *dis*like you." It turned out he was only hanging around me to get closer to one of my friends. I didn't date for a while after that.

And here Linny is, turning down guys left and right. *How can I be the slightest bit jealous of a pregnant sixteen-year-old?* I stick a bookmark in the journal and put it on my nightstand. No more reading the journal tonight. It's dredging up too many hard emotions.

My phone rings, and I reach for it on the nightstand. Kerry has been texting me on and off all night because she's reading the journal too. But Brody's smiling face stares back at me.

I may have snagged a picture of him when we went out for pizza that first night. It's his profile, and I'm pretty sure I was stealthy enough to take the picture without him noticing. I've gotten pretty good practice capturing pictures without my brother noticing over the years so I can get him back at embarrassing moments.

I swipe to answer. Brody hasn't called since he left Hank with me, but he texted and sent me GIFs. "Hello, dog pawner offerer."

He chuckles. "I don't think those are actual words."

"You just wait. It will be in the dictionary in another year or two."

"Make sure you get credit." He clears his throat. "How is Hank? You two getting along all right?"

"Lucky for you, your dog is actually well-behaved."

"Told you. He's had all the training. Graduated top of his class."

"Is that even a thing?"

"It should be."

I smile and lean back against my pillow. "So where are you, anyway, that you had to take off and leave your dog?" *Please don't tell me you went on a getaway with a woman.* Because that would totally happen to me. I'd be the woman who babysits the hot guy's dog while the he goes off to seduce some woman.

"Work. I'll be back by the end of the week."

"Work as in... It occurs to me that I don't know exactly what you do other than play the guitar." *Is he playing in bars somewhere?*

"That pretty much sums it up. I fancy it up sometimes and call myself a musician, but I basically play the guitar. And sing. I add some words to the chords sometimes too." He gives a self-deprecating chuckle.

"You're selling yourself short. I'd love to hear you play sometime. Are you going to be performing around Granite Cove at all this summer?"

"I haven't booked anything, but I get antsy if I don't play, so maybe I'll book a gig or two."

"You didn't say where you are."

"Nashville."

"Ooh, I've seen pictures. Are you playing on that street with all the bars?"

"That's the one."

"That's exciting." I can picture him on the stage, strumming his guitar and singing. I bet he's surrounded by women just waiting for him to look their way. An ugly feeling in the pit of my stomach wipes the smile off my face.

I have no right to be jealous. I'm just Brody's best friend's sister. I'm not his girlfriend. We're not even dating. We're... I'm not exactly sure what we are. Friends, I guess.

"It's not really. It used to be, but lately, I've been questioning where this is going and if I want to be doing it in five years."

"Normal questions. As someone who's approaching thirty, I've been asking myself similar ones."

"What did you come up with? And don't forget we have a wedding planned on your thirtieth birthday."

"How could I forget?" I know he's just flirting and it means nothing, but it still makes me warm inside when he does. "I haven't come up with any answers yet, just the questions."

"Are you questioning whether teaching is what you want to do?"

"Among other things. I can't remember ever actually wanting to be a teacher. I tutored in high school, and my teachers said I would make an outstanding teacher one day. I didn't have any other plan, so I majored in education and became a teacher."

"You don't enjoy it?"

"I like it. The kids are great—usually. But I don't know if I have a passion for it like you do your music. And there are better teachers than me at the school."

"Why do you think they're better?"

"They're excited about teaching. They're always coming up with new ways to convey whatever they're attempting to get the kids to learn. I work hard, and I try to do my best, but it's a job to me." My shoulders drop along with my stomach. *Am I a terrible person for saying that?*

"Have you thought of anything else you might try?"

"You mean to help the kids learn?" He's right. I should refocus and try harder.

"No, I mean for a different career path. There are endless possibilities."

"Not really. I mean, I can't leave Granite Cove because Brian and my parents need me. And I love it here. My friends are all here. My friend Lucinda totally reinvented herself. She was a lawyer and is now a wedding planner and part owner of an inn. I know it's possible, but she hated being a lawyer. I don't hate being a teacher. I guess I feel a little stuck."

"You can't live your life for other people, Mon. Your parents can take care of themselves, and Brian is about to be a husband. You're not stuck there unless you want to be. There're these things called planes now. You could visit anytime you wanted."

"I know what you're saying, and I don't disagree, Mr. Sarcasm, but it's not like I have the money to jet off to places either. There's still the need of an income to support myself." I do have responsibilities that I can't disregard. His life isn't mine.

"Is it only money holding you back? Because money isn't hard to come by."

"Says the boy born with the silver spoon in his mouth." I wince. "That was harsher than I intended."

"No, I get it. I grew up with money, but I left that behind when I dropped out of college. I do know how to live without a trust fund."

"I know. I'm sorry. I guess it's a sorer point than I thought. How did we get on this subject anyway? You didn't say what you want to be doing in your life."

"Sure I did. I'm marrying you on your thirtieth birthday."

There go those butterflies again. "Very funny."

"I'm still trying to figure out the answers to those questions too. Maybe we should talk some more and figure them out together. Two heads are better than one, right?"

"Not the worst idea you've ever had."

"The worst idea might've been crashing my dad's Porsche when I wasn't supposed to be driving it."

"Oh? You meant to do that?"

"Now who's being funny. And I may not have meant to crash it, but I sure as hell meant to piss him off. I just wish I had come up with a better way to do it. It's definitely in the top ten of my regrets. How about you? What do you regret?"

Rosie's smiling face flashes behind my eyes.

"I regret believing my mother when she said brussels sprouts tasted like cheese and would improve my vision."

Brody laughs. "Not a fan of brussels sprouts, huh?"

"Hate them. And they may have some vitamins or minerals in there because they sure taste like dirt, but no amount of cheese on top is enough for me to eat them again. Ew!"

"That's a strong reaction to something you're not even eating at the moment. Remind me to never feed you any."

"Your dog just licked my toe. And why didn't you warn me he likes sleeping under the covers? I never heard of such a thing. I was afraid he was going to suffocate the first time. But every time, he stares at me until I let him under."

"I never thought I'd be jealous of my dog."

# Chapter Eleven

"How *dare* they?" Dad paces the kitchen with a scowl etched on his face. His clenched fists bump against his legs as he pivots and makes another circuit.

Mom sniffles at the kitchen table while holding a tissue under her nose like she's praying.

*How am I going to fix this?*

*Did Brian know his future mother-in-law was going to show up at our parents' house and accuse them of taking financial advantage of her, not wanting Brian and Katy to get married, not caring enough or supporting Brian?*

No, Brian knows how fragile Mom is. He knows Dad would not handle it well. I watch him pace. *Do I have to worry about his blood pressure? His heart?*

There's no way my brother knew about this ambush, but he had to have heard Katy's parents ranting about Mom and Dad before this. A person doesn't get to this point of a tirade without making her feelings clear to those around her beforehand. Brian has let it slip that Katy's parents are overly critical and controlling. I know he and Katy have had discussions about her parents' lack of boundaries. *Why didn't Brian warn me?*

A better question is why he didn't put them in their place so they wouldn't have the audacity to attack our parents. He couldn't possibly agree with them. Our parents are paying for half of the reception, even though they can't afford it and have had no say in any of the planning. My poor mother had to beg to have Aunt Aggie invited. The woman is closer to us than any actual blood relative. While our side will have one sad table at the reception, the bride's side will fill the rest. They're inviting relatives they don't even speak to and filling the tables with friends and acquaintances. Yet the woman has the nerve to attack my parents and say they're taking financial advantage of them by refusing to pay more. They shouldn't be paying for any of it, since they have no say in the planning and aren't allowed to invite friends and extended family.

My blood pressure spikes, and my heartbeat drums in my ears. I should go over to their house and give them a hefty dose of reality. *And maybe a smack or two.* Not that I condone violence. *Most of the time.*

My parents have always supported Brian in whatever he chose to do. They and I have helped him financially, emotionally, and physically any time he needed. *How dare they say we don't care or support him?*

I glare at the list on the table. Yes, the woman had the nerve to bring along a list with her of all the times they paid for something for Brian. *Who the hell keeps a tally of things they do for a family member? What kind of person does that?* There's less than a dozen items. Half of them cost less than fifty dollars. Three of them are for both Brian and Katy. The other two might be worth seventy-five dollars. So it's a few hundred at best for the entire list. *This is their proof of how much they do for Brian?* I could write one hell of a list if I were as petty as them. It would be well into five figures. If anyone is being taken financially advantage of, it's my parents.

*What horrible people.*

Dad stops and leans against the counter, hanging his head. Mom replaces her tissue with a clean one. They don't deserve this. Brian needs to put his future in-laws in their place, or I will. I swipe the list of the table and tear it to shreds. Mom and Dad both look up.

"They're small-minded, selfish, rude, low-class, judgmental jack-asses. They aren't worth a moment more of your time. You've gone above and beyond and tolerated more than anyone should have to." *Karma is a bitch, and it will come for them—someday.*

"I have half a mind to refuse to pay for any of it. They made all the arrangements. They invited the entire guest list. If they can't afford it, it's on them." Dad slaps the counter.

"How are we going to get past this? How are we supposed to go to our son's wedding surrounded by their family? You know if they're saying this to our faces, they're saying even worse behind our backs to everyone. It was bad enough knowing we can't have our family and friends there, but now, after this?" Mom sobs into her hands.

"Son of a bitch!"

My eyes about pop out of my head. My father doesn't swear. At least he never does it in front of us.

"I'll take care of it."

Both their gazes land on me.

I swallow and paste a smile on my face. "Don't worry about it. Everything will be fine." *Yeah, sure, no problem. I can perform miracles.*

"How?" Dad stares at me with a cross between disbelief and hope.

I widen my smile, injecting as much reassurance and confidence as I'm physically capable of. I hope I don't look like a deranged clown. "Simple. With calm reasoning." *Sure, and if you believe that one, I can also single-handedly cure cancer and bring about world peace too.*

My father walks over and clasps my shoulders, nods once, and hugs me. My mother is waiting next to me for her turn when he lets go.

I can't let them down. Somehow, I have to smooth all of this over. I keep the smile pasted on my face all the way out the door and into my car.

I could hop on a flight to Australia and start over, making an entirely new life. *I might need a passport first.*

I pull out of their driveway, and my entire body deflates as I drive down the road. My head wants to drop to the steering wheel, but then I'd probably crash, and more problems would arise. *Unless I got amnesia.* Then I wouldn't have to deal with any of my problems anymore.

My phone ringing echoes through my car, and I glance at the display. *Please don't let it be another problem.*

It's Lucinda. She might have news about the author of the journal.

"Hi, Lucinda."

"Hi. Is this a good time?"

"Depends. Do you have good news or bad news?" It's not fair to expose her to my drama. "Just kidding. What do you need?"

"What's wrong?"

"Nothing." I try to inject some cheer into my voice. "Do you have news about the journal? I haven't finished it yet, so no spoilers, please."

"Monica, talk to me. I can tell you're upset. Your voice is tight."

So much for faking good cheer. *What am I supposed to say?* I can't drag Lucinda into my family drama.

Although she is a wedding planner. She might have experience dealing with troublesome people. In fact, I know she does. I've heard some of her bridezilla and mother-of-the-bride nightmare stories. "What would you advise when the parents of the bride are awful human beings who verbally attacked and ambushed the groom's parents?" I fill her in on some of the details and end with my promise to handle it for my parents.

"Wow. You sure you want to take that on? Usually, what gets people through the planning of a wedding is if they can put their own feelings aside and do what's best for their child, who they hopefully love enough. You really have to love a sibling to do it for them."

"Says the woman who handled her sister's wedding and mother so Franny could have a beautiful wedding without her mother destroying her peace."

"Yes, well, I love my sister and would do anything for her. Including enduring our mother's selfish, narcissistic tantrums. Do you love your brother that much? Because as I see it, you have three choices. One, bite your tongue until after the wedding. Two, tell them to go to hell and that you'll pay nothing if they don't change their attitude and make the wedding about both sides, not just theirs. Three, have a sit-down with them and talk about boundaries, respect, and fairness. Of course, I don't know the bride's parents, so you'll have to decide whether they have the emotional maturity, intelligence, or common decency to have a rational discussion. Some people are incapable of seeing anyone's needs but their own. Unfortunately, it sounds like your brother's future in-laws might lean to the latter."

Sighing, I pull into my driveway, park, and lean my head on the steering wheel. "They definitely lean toward the latter." Biting our tongues would probably be the easiest, but I promised my parents I'd fix this. So number one is out. If Dad had his way, number two would be the choice, but it'll be me demanding their attitude change. And it will probably only make everything worse because they're awful people incapable of thinking about anyone but themselves. I know number three won't work because—see number two.

"I'm so screwed."

"What can I do to help? Want to have an emergency book-club meeting? I'm sure once the ladies get their heads together, we can come up with something."

"If Aunt Aggie finds out about this, she'll start World War III with Katy's parents. It won't help." I love my godmother, but she tends to be impulsive and over-the-top.

"So we won't include Aggie this time." Lucinda laughs. "Although I like the image of her storming off to battle. I can totally see her doing an epic battle cry as she lays siege to their home."

A smile wobbles across my lips. "She would." I sigh. A fourth possibility just occurred to me. It goes against the grain because it gives Katy's parents what they want. Inappropriate behavior shouldn't be rewarded. But what Lucinda said about loving Brian enough to handle this stuck in my head. I do. If I come up with the money, then my parents will be left alone, and Brian will get married in peace—hopefully not knowing how awful his future in-laws truly are.

"Thanks, Lucinda. I know what I need to do now." It's going to be painful and drain my savings for a vacation that I've been dreaming about for years. But I can delay it another year.

"Are you sure? I can start a text string in the blink of an eye and have the ladies brainstorm a solution that might be without bloodshed."

"I'm sure, but thanks for being my sounding board."

"Any time."

"Oh, what were you calling about?"

"How far are you in the journal?"

"Pregnant."

"Oh good, then I'm not spoiling anything for you. I had a thought.

Since the journal was buried here in Granite Cove, the odds are high that Linny was a student here, right?"

"I guess, but she could've been a summer person or here on vacation. I haven't read anything in the journal that says she lives in Granite Cove. Have you?"

"Shoot. No, she's really vague with details like that. Nevertheless, if she were a student here and a pregnant one at that, wouldn't there be a record somewhere in the school system?"

"I suppose it's likely that the guidance counselor or school psychologist might've made notes about it if they spoke to her. Lucinda, you're not asking me to get access to those records, are you? Not only would it be illegal, but I work at the elementary school, not the high school and don't have access."

"Hmm. Kerry works at the high school."

"Lucinda, you're a former lawyer. You're not going to ask Kerry to break into the school records, right?"

"Of course not! I would never tell someone to break the law. But if she happened to need to see certain records for a legitimate reason, that wouldn't be illegal."

"Why would she need to look at records at least two decades or more old?"

"Well, that's going to require a little more thought."

I squeeze my eyes shut. "How about we exhaust all our research avenues before we contemplate the quasi-legal ones?"

"We'll talk again when you finish reading the journal. I have this burning desire to make sure Linny gets justice, and I bet my new shoes you will too. And I really like these shoes."

# Chapter Twelve

The numbers are not only doubling and tripling, but they're also doing a sideways dance on the page. It might be time to take a break. My eyes are dry and sore and feel like someone tried to scoop them out with a spoon. Okay, that one might've been from the horror film I was too terrified to change the channel away from. Besides, it's not like the numbers are getting any better or an answer is going to leap off the page any minute. I've been trying to figure out a solution to the wedding problem for three hours. Even emptying my savings isn't going to cover it all. I'll have to cut back on expenses somewhere. *But where?* I have one television subscription service, which came free with my phone, which I only upgraded because my last one literally died and refused to be revived. I get my hair cut at the local college by the hairdressers in training and only twice a year. I suppose I could start unplugging all my appliances when I'm not using them. I saw a video once that says it works. My only other option is to cut back on my and my parents' groceries. *How am I going to explain that without them wondering why I can't buy them that steak they had a craving for?*

The questions will come, and I suck at lies.

Hank woofs at the door as headlights shine through the window.

"Good guard doggy."

I peek out the window and spot a familiar Jeep. Brody's back. I look down at the dog. That means Hank is leaving. A weight sinks into the pit of my stomach. I got too attached in just a few days. I knew it would happen. I have no self-control when it comes to pets.

Hank does his adorable tilted-head thing that makes me believe he's reading my mind. *Would Brody notice if I dognapped his dog?* It's his own fault for leaving him with me.

The knock on the door makes me jump. Dognapping isn't in the cards for me, especially since I have to cut back on my groceries. Maybe Brody will let me have visitation rights—at least while he's in Granite Cove for the summer.

Brody smiles when I open the door. His dimple hasn't popped out, so it's not a full grin. In fact, his smile is a little wobbly. *Did something go wrong in Nashville?*

My gaze lands on a duffel bag resting against his leg. *Did he come straight from the airport?* He must've missed Hank a lot. That's another reason I can't dognap Hank. "How was your trip?"

"Fine." He scratches the back of his neck, then his gaze drops as Hank pushes his way between my legs and the door. *I wasn't blocking him or anything. I was totally blocking him.* "Hey, boy." Brody squats and gives Hank a full-body rub while Hank places his paws on Brody's shoulders.

Brody shifts his focus to me. "I need another favor."

A spark of joy detonates inside me. "Sure. I can watch him a little longer." *Did I answer too quickly? Did it come across as nonchalantly as I planned?*

"That's not exactly the favor. Well, I guess it is part of the favor."

I wave a hand at the bugs circling. Standing outside in the evening with lights on either side of us, and we might as well be holding a sign for the mosquitoes that says it's snack time. "Why don't you come in and explain?"

Hank jumps up to his usual spot on the couch and lies down. Brody drops the bag inside the door and looks around.

"Did you eat dinner? I have some leftover pasta." It was totally going to be my lunch for the next couple of days, but it's a worthy sacrifice if I'm going to get Hank for a little while longer.

"I grabbed something on the way." He rubs the back of his neck then puts his hands on his hips. "The lake house flooded. Any chance I can stay with you until I can get it fixed or find a long-term rental?"

He's still talking. At least, his lips are still moving, but the buzzing in my ears drowns out any words he might be saying. *Brody wants to move in? With me?*

"Never mind. It's too much to ask. I can bunk in a motel until I can find a place that takes pets. You okay with keeping Hank a few more days?" He picks up his duffel.

*A motel?* A hotel would be a better idea. The closest motel is at least forty minutes away and not a place I'd ever willingly sleep in. But Brody has been staying in his parents' house rent free. He probably doesn't have much money to waste on a hotel for however long it takes to repair his parents' house.

"You can stay here." The words are out of my mouth before I can think them through. *Have I completely lost my mind?*

He drops the duffel and grins. This time, his dimples come out. "You sure? I promise to pay rent and pick up after myself, and I can cook too."

Heck, if he follows through on that promise, it might help solve my wedding financial problem. *Definitely too good to be true.* "Since when do you cook or clean?"

He winks at me. "I've learned a lot over the years."

*Translation: various women have taught him. Along with plenty of other things I don't want to think about.*

Brody picks up his duffel again. "I can bunk with Hank on the couch."

"I have a guest room." *More like there's a bed in my office-slash-exercise-room-slash-library-slash-catchall-room.*

"Great. You sure it's not too much of a bother?"

I can't very well kick him out now. Brian and Katy have a couch. It may be half the size of mine and wouldn't fit Brody's torso, let alone legs, but Brian is his best friend. And Brody is here for Brian's wedding. I can't ask him to do that. I point at the hallway. "First door on the left."

Brody walks down the hallway. He's going to be right next door.

We'll be sharing a wall. I glance at the first door on the right. We'll be sharing a bathroom too.

*Bathroom! Where I left my bras hanging to dry!* I run in there and yank my bras off the shower rod, toss them into my bedroom, and close the door. *Is there anything in the guest room I have to worry about?* I poke my head in. Brody has dropped his bag next to the bed—which is covered in books.

"Sorry!" I grab a handful of books and put them in front of the overflowing bookshelves taking up the far wall. *Maybe they'll help hamper any sounds between our rooms. One can hope.*

"No worries."

I turn, and Brody is looking at the covers of the books he's holding. *Of course they would be the romance books with half-naked men on the covers.* My cheeks heat. *If he makes one disparaging comment, I'm tossing him and his duffel bag to the curb. Hank can stay.*

"Think I've read this one." He reads the back cover.

"You read romance?"

"Sure. I read just about everything. A friend got me hooked a few years back." He turns to the bookshelves. "You mind if I read a few?"

"Be my guest." *Brody reads romance books.* I might've slipped into an alternate reality. I don't know any men who read romance books. Though I do know a lot of men who should. They might learn something.

# Chapter Thirteen

I kneel onto the folded yoga mat I placed next to Rosie's grave. Too many wet knees and bottoms have taught me a lesson. Besides, my yoga mat isn't getting any use otherwise. I bought it with the best intentions, but time and motivation are scarce.

"Hi, Rosie." I touch the gravestone briefly and sit back on my heels. My pants stretch across my thighs.

*Twenty years.* Today marks the twentieth anniversary of when we all lost our light. None of our lives were the same after that day. Sometimes, I think I'm still that nine-year-old girl who lost her other half, like I've been frozen in time and unable to grow up. Obviously, things have changed. Physically, I'm twenty-nine. Mentally might be up for debate, depending on the day. But emotionally, that scared, devastated little girl still exists inside me. She's curled up in a ball in the middle of her bed, staring at the empty one across from hers, knowing it will always be empty no matter what she does.

A breeze rustles the leaves budding along the branches of the trees and lifts my hair against my neck. The flowers I planted have bloomed, and the pinks pop against the headstone.

"I think my kids are already transitioning into summer mode, even though there's a month left of school. I got a lot of blank stares today, and they keep staring out the window like they're planning a jailbreak." *That last one might've been me. I might have been counting the hours until the day was done and planning an escape.*

"Guess who has a tall, gorgeous roommate." I pluck a dead petal off a flower. "How do I get myself into these things, Rosie?" *Oh yeah, I don't say no. I just smile and nod.*

"As far as roommates go, he's off to a pretty good start, though. Before I left for work, he made me breakfast and packed me a lunch, and the kitchen and bathroom were spotless. He even asked if I had a preference for dinner. If he keeps this up, I might not let him leave."

Aaron and I never lived together, but he barely knew how to turn on a stove, and he certainly never made me a meal or packed me a lunch. He never even picked up his apartment before I came over. Those should have been giant red flags that our relationship was going nowhere. A guy needs to show some effort if he cares about you. Not that Brody cares about me in that way. He's just trying to say thanks for letting him and Hank stay.

"Brian's wedding plans have hit some snags." *More like roadblocks or tanks and explosives, but I'm trying to keep a positive spin on this for my sanity.* "Katy's parents are difficult." *Translation: they're pure evil.* "Don't worry, though. I've promised Mom and Dad I'll take care of it. Brian is going to get his happily ever after." *Even if I have to go into debt, sell a kidney, or bury a body.*

*That last one shouldn't perk me up like it does. I might need to seek therapy again. Because it was so successful in the past. Inner eye roll on steroids happening here.*

I slump forward. "I'm so tired, Rosie. I'm trying to do the right things and keep everyone happy, but it doesn't seem to be working. Things keep going wrong, and I can't keep juggling everything."

I rub my hands over my pants and stare up at the trees swaying lightly in the breeze. "Sometimes, I don't even know who I am anymore. I'm a daughter, sister, friend, and teacher. But is that all? There's this emptiness inside me, and sometimes I feel it's growing, and it's going to swallow me whole." I shift to the side, sit on my bottom, and pull my knees into my chest. "Look at me getting all melancholy and dramatic.

You were the dramatic one, remember? I was supposed to be the calm one."

Hammering and sawing echo from a nearby development. *Another house going up or renovations on someone's dream home?* Cars drive by on the road behind me. It's a little early for summer people to arrive, but traffic has already picked up in town.

"Have I told you about the journal my book club is reading? I finally finished it late last night." I wasn't getting any sleep, imagining Brody on the other side of the wall and listening for any sound coming from the guest room.

"It was sad, but it also made me laugh at parts because Linny is funny. She's so raw. She doesn't pull any punches and acknowledges her mistakes." I pick at the grass. "It made me feel lacking because I'm always biting my tongue instead of saying what I want to say. I don't own up to my mistakes either. I hide instead.

"I wonder what would happen if I just started saying what I was thinking to everyone. Sometimes, I imagine it in my head. It's mildly satisfying, but I know I can't do that for real. I'd really like to tell Katy's parents what I think about them for how they've behaved, but that would only hurt Brian, so I can't."

It would make me as bad as them. Okay, maybe not quite as bad, because they are awful, but it probably wouldn't make them behave any better. But they might realize they can't get away with being so hateful and selfish anymore.

Linny called her sister on her horrible behavior, and it didn't make her change. She also told the dick who got her pregnant what she thought of him. It didn't get her what she wanted. But it made her feel good for a while. Maybe if she had kept her mouth closed and bit her tongue, things would've turned out differently for her. She wouldn't have had the satisfaction, but she might've had something far more precious.

"Linny was a teenage mother, but she didn't let it break her. It almost did, but she yanked herself out of the hole she'd crawled into. Then they took her baby from her."

Lucinda said once I read the whole journal, I'd want justice for Linny, and she was right. I want to track them all down.

The journal ended after they took Linny's son away from her. I don't know if any of them are still alive or what happened to them. But I intend to find out.

"The book-club ladies and I have been texting, and we're all committed to unraveling the mystery of Linny and her baby. You'd like them, Rosie. I know I've said that before, but it's true. You'd probably be leading the charge to find out who Linny is and what happened to her. You were always fearless. You and Lucinda would hit it off. She's the one doing the leading."

I dust away the pile of grass I've plucked into my lap. "You might've gotten all the good genes in the womb." Rosie was prettier, funner, brave, and talented. Everyone loved her, including me—especially me.

After standing, I roll up the yoga mat and tuck it under my arm.

"I'm sorry I failed you, Rosie. I should've been a better sister. If I could go back and change it, I would. It's my biggest regret." *My biggest shame.*

Tears spill out of my eyes as I walk toward my car at the front of the cemetery. I wish I'd parked closer today. But I was trying to be considerate of other visitors and not block the driveway.

A pair of shoes and legs appear in my line of vision. *Has Brian or Dad decided to visit Rosie today?* Brian only goes on our birthday because it's expected. I'm not sure when or if Dad goes. I glance up, and my entire body clenches.

*Not Brian or Dad. Paul Swift.*

I'd know him anywhere, even if it has been twenty years and I was a child at the time. He's completely gray with a beard and skinnier. He appears haggard, like the last twenty years haven't been kind.

Paul gives me a slight nod and continues walking toward me. His gaze goes beyond me then snaps back as recognition dawns. "Monica?"

Perspiration breaks out on my skin, even though it's only sixty-five degrees today and breezy. My brain scrambles for words, but they won't come. I've imagined this day for years—confronting him. Sometimes, I screamed and hit him. Other times, I watched him be led away in handcuffs because the police realized they made a mistake and it wasn't an accident. Not one of those times did I imagine I would be struck mute.

Tears fill his eyes slide down his cheeks. "I'm so sorry," he whispers.

I glance away and stare at the clouds until my eyes dry. I should walk straight to my car and drive away without a word. *Who cares if he's sorry? Who cares if the guilt has weighed on him? Shouldn't it? He was driving the car. He lived.*

"I know there aren't any words to make it better. I'm not asking for forgiveness."

*Damn well better not be.* I grip the yoga mat against my chest.

"I only want you to know I've never forgotten. I'll never forget. I'd do anything to change the outcome of that day."

*Me too.*

*How many times have I said those same words?* I glance at him. He's staring at the sad-looking bunch of pink and lavender flowers clutched in his hand. I've seen similar pink and lavender bouquets left at Rosie's grave over the years. *Did he leave them?*

*Why do I hate him so much? Why have I blamed him?* Maybe he could've been a better driver, or maybe he did everything he could've. *Would I have felt any better if he or Holly had died too?*

*No.*

Rosie should never have been in the car. The blame for that is mine.

"It wasn't your fault," I whisper.

His gaze shoots up to mine and widens like he can't believe the words that came out of my mouth.

*Me either.*

We stare at each other silently for what feels like an hour, but it is probably only a moment. Time really hasn't been kind to him. He's suffered enough for something that was truly an accident. It could've been anyone driving that car.

His mouth makes some sort of weird spasm, like he's trying to smile but has forgotten how. "I started drinking after the accident—had a hard time dealing with the guilt." He rubs his hand across his mouth. "Got divorced. Didn't see Holly much after that."

A boulder lodges in my stomach. *Why is he telling me this? What am I supposed to say?* Everyone involved was affected and dealt with their grief in different ways—mostly negatively. *Well, except Holly and Nancy. They seem fine.* I wince. *Not fair.* I don't know what they've been through. I didn't know Paul and Nancy divorced or that Holly grew up without her dad.

"I've been sober for six months, and part of the program is to make amends. I'm doing my best to do that with Nancy and Holly." He smiles slightly. "She's getting married, and I want to be there. Won't be the one to walk her down the aisle. That'll be her stepdad." He shakes his head. "My point is I haven't gotten up the nerve to make amends to your family yet. Don't want to make things worse for them. Bring up terrible memories. It was before I started drinking, but I couldn't make myself go to the funeral back then. Do you think... Would it do more harm to pay my respects to your parents now?"

*Is my mouth gaping open?* I press my lips tightly together and breathe deeply through my nose. "I don't think that's a good idea." *More like a terrible idea.*

He doesn't react, just stares at the ground.

"It's just that my mom... It's still really hard for both of them."

"I understand. I'll stay away."

*Am I doing the right thing?* Maybe I should ask Mom's therapist what he thinks. I thought she'd have another breakdown after that run-in with Holly and Nancy, but she didn't. Perhaps she's stronger than I think. Maybe it might help her. I certainly don't have the answers. My parents were friends with the Swifts before the accident.

"Let me think about it. Test the waters. If you give me your number and they're receptive to the idea, I'll call. Okay?" *Who am I, and what alternate reality have I stepped into?* If someone had told me I would not only speak to Paul Swift but ask for his number so he might talk to my parents, I would've told them they were insane. *But who am I to decide what's best for my parents?*

My lungs empty of air in a whoosh. It's like I slipped an overweight backpack from my shoulders. The knot in my stomach unwinds. Paul Swift was the enemy in my head for so long. When something so tragically life changing occurs, we need someone to blame—even if no one *is* to blame.

He gives me his number, and I program it into my phone. "Thank you, Monica. I can't tell you what today means to me. Seeing you here.

Talking to you." He shakes his head as tears fill his eyes again. "It means a lot."

"Twenty years is a long time. We all have our demons." *Some of us more than others.* "I'm glad I ran into you." As I say the words, I realize they're sincere. "And you may not have asked for my forgiveness, but you have it."

He hangs his head, and a sob shakes his spare frame.

I touch his arm as I pass. Whoever said holding on to anger only harms yourself was right. Letting go of the anger and blame I placed on him is freeing.

*Now if I could only forgive myself.*

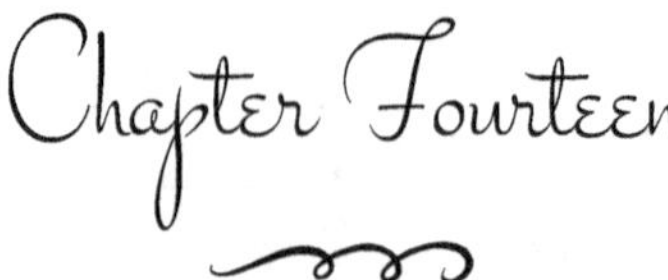

# Chapter Fourteen

Music drifts toward me as I climb out of my car—a guitar and a soulful, smooth voice. *Is that Brody?*

I shut my door as quietly as I can and inch closer to the front door. His voice wraps around me like a warm blanket on a chilly night. *How did I not know he could sing so well? Why isn't he famous?*

I can't play an instrument and don't know the first thing about being a musician, but the notes he plays are beautiful. It's like he's making the guitar cry and laugh to go along with the words he's singing about a man falling in love for the first time.

The music drifts off after a sweet melody. I press my ear to the door, waiting to see if he's going to play something else. Disappointment crashes over me when he doesn't. Maybe I should make it a condition of his rent. He has to serenade me a minimum of three times a week.

He's sitting on the couch when I open the door. "Hey." His grin lights up his face and a place in my chest that I refuse to analyze too closely.

"Hi. That sounded so beautiful. I had no idea you're so talented."

*Is that a blush on Brody Jackson's face?* It just might be.

"Thanks."

"I hope you'll play some more." I bend down to pet Hank, who came over to greet me.

Brody rests his guitar against the couch. "Later. I made dinner. It's warming in the oven. I hope you like meatloaf." He stands and stretches.

I try valiantly not to stare at the strip of skin revealed on his abdomen.

"I like pretty much anything I don't have to cook." I hang up my coat and drop my tote on the floor. "Just give me a few minutes to wash up." *And get my heart rate under control and make sure there isn't any drool on my chin.*

When I come out of the bathroom, he's already got the table set and pulls a pan out of the oven with meatloaf and vegetables. *I could get used to this.*

*And that is exactly the problem. This is temporary.*

"Anything left for me to do?"

He smiles and shakes his head. "Just have a seat."

My phone rings as I pull out a chair and he places the food on the table. It's Brian. I bite my lip. "Sorry. I have to take this." Otherwise, he'll think something is wrong because he knows what this day usually does to me.

Brody waves his hand. "Go ahead."

I step away from the table. "Hey, Brian."

I feel Brody's gaze on me. He's probably concerned something is wrong with his friend. I toss a smile in his direction and turn to the window.

"Are you home?"

"Yeah. Just walked in the door."

"So you went already? Everything is good?"

"Yes, but there is something we need to discuss."

"Is it Mom or Dad?"

That's a normal question, since this anniversary is always hard on the family. "Neither, actually. Not directly anyway. As I was leaving the cemetery, I ran into Paul Swift. He was visiting Rosie and leaving flowers."

"What the fuck! Did he see you? Why didn't you call me? Tell me that asshole didn't say anything to you!"

I pivot closer to the corner of the room and pray Brody can't hear Brian's tirade. He never said anything to make me think he felt so strongly about Paul Swift. Then again, it's not like we openly discussed the Swifts or anything to do with the past.

Hank whines at my feet, and as I glance down, I see Brody has followed me across the room with concern etched on his face. I smile and mouth, "It's fine."

"Brian, please calm down. If you saw what he looks like, you'd have a hard time being mad at him. I know I did."

"Who cares what he looks like?"

"He looks like hell. Haggard."

"Good. He should be dead."

"Bri." *Can I really blame him?* I felt the same often enough. "He's suffered. It was an accident. How would you feel if you had been the one driving? I thought about how I would feel, and it made me physically ill. He told me he started drinking after the accident and got divorced."

"So the bastard did talk to you."

"Yes, and at first, I admit I was angry with him too. But what point does it serve? Haven't we all been punished enough? I'm so tired of being angry. Especially at someone just because they were lucky enough to survive."

The heat of Brody's body behind me makes me want to lean back. He settles his hands on my shoulders.

"He's sober and trying to make amends to his family and us. Blaming him is like blaming the deer or the tree. It's pointless."

"He'd better not go near Mom and Dad."

"Again, that was my initial reaction, too, but what if we're wrong? What if it might help them? They were good friends with the Swifts before the accident. We should ask Mom's therapist for his opinion."

"You can talk to the therapist, but don't bring it up with Mom or Dad. You know they can't handle anything like that. I'm getting married. I'd like my parents there and not in an institution or completely checked out of reality."

I squeeze my eyes shut. I tried so hard to make sure Brian had a happy childhood and wasn't affected by our parents' spirals after the accident. I guess I failed. Of course I did. He lived in the same house and knew what was happening, so he had to be affected.

"Okay, we'll table this until after the wedding. A few more months won't make a difference."

"Thank you. Are you sure you're okay?"

"Yes, I'm good. I'll talk to you later, and I'm sorry for upsetting you."

"You didn't. I just wish all the reminders would go away. I get why you feel the need to go to the cemetery, but it's not the same for me."

"I know, and that's okay. It helps me."

"Okay. Love you."

"Love you too."

After I hang up, Brody squeezes my shoulders. "What can I do?"

I shake my head and will the tears away.

"Today's the anniversary of the accident, isn't it?"

I nod.

"I'm sorry. I didn't realize."

"Why would you? It's fine. I'd really like to just sit and enjoy the nice dinner you made, okay?"

"We can do that."

I turn and smile at him. "Thank you."

We sit, and he serves both of us. I take a bite and pause. My gaze shoots to his. "This is really good."

He chuckles. "I see you doubted my abilities."

"No, not exactly. It's just the men in my life aren't all that great in the kitchen. Although my friend Rebecca's husband is the chef in their relationship, and he owns the pub in town." I point at my plate as I take another bite. "Meatloaf has never been high on my dining choices, but this is really good."

We eat in silence for several minutes as I replay the phone conversation in my head. "Was I wrong? About talking to Paul Swift, telling Brian about it, and considering talking to my mom's therapist?"

He stares at me for a moment then shakes his head. "I think you're right about letting go of the anger. It sounds like it was an accident. He wasn't drinking and driving. He wasn't texting or otherwise distracted. He swerved to avoid a deer and hit a tree. What you said about it could've been anyone driving is true. I've done some stupid shit behind the wheel of a car. Thank god I never hurt anyone. I doubt I could live with myself if I had. It sounds like Swift hasn't been able to deal with it, either, and it wasn't even his fault."

I drop my fork and rub my forehead. "I was so angry with him for so long. I knew he wasn't to blame, but I guess he was a convenient target. Doesn't say much for me as a person, does it?"

Brody reaches across the table and takes my hand. "You're one of the best people I know. Don't beat yourself up over something that's completely understandable. You were a kid. Adults would have a hard time getting past something like that."

"I told him I forgave him."

"I'm sure that helped him tremendously. See? One of the best people I know."

I shake my head as my eyes fill with tears. "I'm not. The accident wasn't his fault. It was mine. Rosie was only in that car because of me." I drop my head as the tears fall down my cheeks.

Brody's hand leaves mine.

He's appalled. Of course he is. I'm a horrible person.

His hands wrap around me, and I blink at him squatting next to me.

"Monica, the accident wasn't your fault. Have you been blaming yourself all this time?"

"It was. Mom was supposed to drive us both to gymnastics, but she had to stay home and watch me because I was sick. That's the only reason Rosie went with the Swifts." I shudder and gasp for breath between sobs. "I wasn't sick. I lied. I wanted to stay home with our new pet bunny we got for our birthday."

Brody lifts me out of the chair and carries me to the couch. I'm draped over his lap, sobbing into his shoulder. He rubs my back and holds me tightly against him.

Eventually, my sobs lessen into hiccups.

Brody cups my cheek against his shoulder. "Mon, would you blame Rosie if she were the one to stay home with the bunny? How many times did she fake an illness to get out of something? Kids do it all the time. You're a teacher. How many times have you seen a kid fake a stomachache or cough to get out of school? Would you blame them if something indirectly happened after they did that? Do you blame your mom for not keeping Rosie home instead of letting her go with the Swifts? So many different choices could've been made, and it makes no sense to blame everyone for innocent decisions. Every day, we all make hundreds of choices and decisions. It's like dominos. It was an accident. No one is to blame. Certainly not you, a nine-year-old kid."

Rosie did fake a tummy ache to stay home when she wanted to. I got the idea from watching her. I even did her signature move of moaning and rubbing my tummy while curled up in a ball. But nothing bad happened when she pretended to be sick.

Of course I wouldn't blame one of my students if something bad happened as a result of their faking an illness or fibbing about something else.

But none of it feels the same in my head. His words make sense, but they don't make the guilt lessen.

Brody leans forward with me still in his arms and picks up the box of tissues from the table. I take one from him and wipe my face. I should probably climb out of his lap, but I don't want to. It's been so long since I've been held.

He kisses the top of my head. "Did Brian ever tell you about the time he visited me in New York?"

I shake my head.

"It was before I dropped out of college. He was supposed to stay the week, but I told him I had a paper to write, so he ended up leaving a day early. The truth was I had a fight with my parents and didn't want him to witness the fallout. What if something had happened to Brian when he left early? Would you have blamed me if the train had derailed or he'd gotten in a car accident on the way home from the train station?"

"Of course not."

"The only difference was you were a child and I was an adult."

"Would you have blamed yourself?"

"Maybe for a while." He tilts his head toward me. "But then I'd like to think I'd have someone who cares about me point out how futile it was to blame myself for something that was out of my control."

"You're pretty smart, Mr. Jackson. Was psychology your major before you dropped out?"

He chuckles. "I majored in doing as little as possible."

"Thank you. I've never told anyone about pretending to be sick."

He stares at me with a slight tilt to his lips, and his hazel eyes search mine for something.

*Is he trying to figure out if I'm okay? Or maybe he's staring at the remnants of my makeup, which is probably smeared all over. Or my puffy face.*

Hank jumps onto the couch next to me and sticks his cold, wet nose in my face. I laugh and rub his head.

"Is that the reason you don't have any pets? Because it's obvious you love Hank."

I shrug. "Self-imposed punishment."

"Rosie wouldn't have blamed you."

"I know, but it's hard to let go of the guilt and shame."

"Maybe it's time to forgive yourself like you forgave Swift. Punishing yourself by denying yourself the love of a pet isn't going to help anyone. It's okay to live, Monica."

"I live." I have friends. I shift off his lap and cuddle Hank.

Brody puts his arm along the back of the couch and my shoulders. "Denying yourself what you want and putting everyone else's needs before your own isn't truly living. You have nothing to atone for."

*Is that how he really sees me? Is that what I've been doing?* I suppose from his point of view, it might look that way. I've never left Granite Cove. *Why haven't I?*

My parents and Brian need me. And I've always felt like it should've been me instead of Rosie.

# Chapter Fifteen

"Monica, you have a moment?" Lisette has taken her new vice principal position very seriously and expects everyone else to as well. She stands in the door of her new office, waiting for me. It would probably never occur to her I would refuse. When she was a teacher here, she acted like she was better than the rest of us. Now that she's got a modicum of power, she's become even more insufferable.

"Sure, Lisette." It's not like the day is over and I have other things to do.

"Ms. Grover, please."

Right, we're supposed to forget she was a teacher here and know her by her first name. While she continues to use ours, we're supposed to be more formal and use her last name.

I say nothing and slip past her into her small office. It's about the size of a walk-in closet, but she has a desk, two chairs, and an assortment of framed certificates and awards on the wall behind her.

"I've been reviewing your file and—"

"Why?" She's in charge of student activities, discipline, and some of the administration tasks. I know because I briefly considered getting my master's degree and applying for the position when I heard Carol was planning to retire this year. If I had known Lisette would get the position, maybe I would've made a different decision.

"Because it's my job to make sure the school and all its staff perform at top levels. If there are weak areas, it brings us all down."

*Since when am I a weak area?* I've been a teacher here for six years—more if you count the years I interned or substituted.

She points at one of the frames on the wall. "Do you see this award? I got it for my perfect attendance as a teacher."

*Is that a real thing?* I thought only students got those. Wait, they don't even give those to students anymore because it encourages kids to come to school sick and spread germs.

"You've never gotten one, have you?" She glances at her computer screen. "I see you have many absences." Her long nails tap on her desk in a broken rhythm that makes the back of my neck twitch.

*You should take that award and stick it where the sun don't shine.* "I wouldn't say many, and every single one was using my sick or personal days." It's not like I'm just not showing up or taking days I don't have.

"Sick days are for legitimate illnesses, not for social visits. I believe your last one you spent with your mother."

I grip the arms of the chair, still my tapping foot. *Social visit?* My mother had a cancer scare. She needed a PET scan, and the only appointments available were during the day. I love my dad, but he is useless with medical concerns. She needed me to take her. Then of course I had to take her to the follow-up appointment. Luckily, she doesn't have cancer. I stand. "Personal days are just that—personal. If you have any more questions or comments, I'll be sure to have my union rep present." *And you can go straight to hell!*

The metal doorknob is cold in my hand as I yank open the heavy door and stalk out of her office. I glance down to make sure my body isn't really shaking as hard as it feels like it is.

Completely on automatic, I reach my car and drive out of the parking lot. I can't break down at school. Not only do I not want to give Lisette the satisfaction, but I also don't want anyone to witness my distress. I need to find somewhere safe to pull over and calm down before I cause an accident, somewhere private and close.

I pull into the parking lot of one of the many hiking trails around town and pray that not too many people got the urge to take a hike this afternoon. Only two other cars are in the lot, and I park on the opposite side from them, facing away from the road. As soon as I put the car in park, I drop my head on the steering wheel. *What the hell was I thinking?* I should've kept my mouth shut and let her have her moment. If I weren't already a target on her hit list, I bet I just put myself smack-dab in the bull's-eye.

*Can she get me fired? Does she even have that kind of power? What the hell am I going to do if I get fired? Will I be able to get another teaching position?*

A knock on my window makes me jump a foot. My seat belt locks and strangles me. Kerry stands outside my car, alternating between frowning and smiling. I hit the window button.

"Hey, you okay? I saw you pull in." She grimaces as she studies my face. "Monica? What's wrong?"

"I think I just really screwed up."

She juts her chin at the door. "Open up. I'm coming in." She jogs around the back of my car, and I hit the unlock button, then she slides into the passenger seat. "Tell me what happened. Do we need to bury a body?"

I chuckle, which was what she intended. "No. Well, on second thought, it might solve the problem for me. But I guess it would be premeditated."

She just smiles encouragingly, like it's perfectly normal to joke about murder. God, I love the book-club ladies. They've kept me sane over the years.

"You know Lisette is the new vice principal at the elementary school, right?"

"Good grief, is she why you're so upset? I guarantee you we can get a whole passel of teachers to help us hide that body."

"Passel?"

She waves a hand dismissively. "I was chatting with Kelly on the phone when I saw your car. I swear she's getting a Southern twang just like her husband's family." She narrows her gaze. "So what did the evil queen do?"

I laugh. "It suits her." I sigh and turn to face her. "She called me into her office as I was leaving today and called me out on using personal days for what she calls 'social visits.'"

Kerry scowls. "What social visits? Didn't you take one to take your mom to the doctor?"

"Two, actually, and those are what she was referring to."

"What a bitch!"

"She even pointed at an attendance award on the wall she received as something I should aspire to."

Kerry rolls her eyes. "That woman is a piece of work." She pats me on the knee. "Lisette's only on a power trip. I wouldn't worry about her."

"Yeah, it probably would've been fine except I stormed out of her office after telling her any future conversations would be with my union rep and that personal days were personal."

Her eyes get really wide, then she holds up her palm. "You're my new hero."

I give her a weak high five. "You don't think she'll make my life hell and find a way to fire me?"

"I don't see how she has a leg to stand on. You put in the request for those days, right? Followed all the protocols?"

"Yes."

"Then she's got nothing. Why did she even bring it up? Wasn't that before she took over the job?"

I nod.

Kerry shakes her head. "Usually, I'm all for giving someone the benefit of the doubt and trying to find the good in someone. But in this case? She's a lost cause. Some people are simply miserable human beings and want to make everyone else miserable too."

I rest my head against the window. "I don't know what came over me. She made me so angry."

"Look, you stood up for yourself. It's not like you punched her or trashed her office. You didn't even scream at her or call her names. You didn't, right?"

"No, I didn't. I may have thought a few less than complimentary things, but I didn't say or do them."

"Then you're fine. And if she launches a smear campaign or does anything else to you, then I'll go with you to file a formal complaint. She won't last long in that position if she's going to abuse it."

"Did I ever tell you I thought about getting my master's and applying for the position?"

"Me too."

"Really? Why didn't you?"

"Because I love teaching, and I would miss the kids. I don't want to do all the administrative stuff. I like being in the classroom and witnessing those light bulb moments when a kid gets the material I'm teaching and is excited about it. How about you? Why didn't you go for it? You'd be great at all that paperwork and schedules."

"Thanks, I guess. It didn't appeal to me either." I purse my lips. "Kerry, have you ever questioned becoming a teacher?"

"Sure. Doesn't everyone periodically question their life choices, especially when they're having a bad day?"

"I suppose." *What if it isn't just on bad days?*

"Sounds like you're questioning it."

I'm questioning everything. "I like teaching. I love the kids. But I'd be lying if I said I don't wonder whether it's just a job to me. Does that make me awful? I mean, you really seem to love teaching. Like it's your calling or something."

"I do love teaching, and no, it doesn't make you awful at all. Monica, you're an outstanding teacher. It's not like you're just going through the motions for a paycheck. And I could name a few who definitely are, and I'm sure you can too."

She's right. I could name some who should find another profession. "Thanks. That makes me feel better."

"But... I also think if there's something that *is* your passion, you should absolutely pursue it. Is there something else you want to do?"

"There's nothing I feel passionate about that could be translated into a career." *Not unless Brody is looking for a new groupie.* Unfortunately, that's not a paying position. And it's not like I have the personality to follow someone around with puppy dog eyes and adoration. Not when those feelings aren't returned, anyway.

*Crap! I'm falling for Brody again, aren't I?*

# Chapter Sixteen

"Is that a dating profile?"

My phone flies through the air as I chuck it across the living room at the sound of Brody's voice over my shoulder. *Succotash! Succotash! Succotash!*

*Think, Monica! I'm checking out the dating app for a friend? Then why is it with my name and picture? Curiosity about how it works? Lame. I'm well aware how it works—poorly. Not that he needs to know that. Research for an imaginary novel I'm not writing? That will only raise a lot more questions, and how will I answer those?*

Any excuse or, let's be honest here, fib, will only dig a deeper hole. There's no shame in online dating. The shame is crushing on my brother's best friend once again, which is what led me to come up with the desperate idea to try online dating again.

"You have something against your phone?" Brody picks up my phone from the floor under the window.

*Right. How am I going to explain throwing my phone across the room?* Half of me wishes it's broken, even though I can't afford to replace it. The other half cringes, hoping the screen isn't stuck on the profile I was building. "You startled me."

"Remind me to duck in the future if your response to being startled is to throw things." Brody sits next to me on the couch and hands me my phone.

The screen is black. *Broken or just blessedly off?*

"So... online dating?"

I close my eyes and rest my head on the back of the sofa. "It seemed like a good idea at the time." I should know better than to be impulsive. It never works out well for me.

"You do a lot of online dating, or is this a first-time thing?"

"I've done it before then deleted my profile and the app." *Honesty is the best policy, right?*

"Never tried it myself. Why did you delete it before?"

*Of course you've never tried it. Why would you? Women probably throw themselves at you every time you walk onto the stage—and walk off it.* Gorgeous guys like Brody only use the apps for hookups, not looking for an actual relationship. At least none that I've ever seen or heard of.

"Because I realized it was pointless after too many bad dates."

"Yet you're making another profile."

"Dating and I have a hate-hate relationship, but every once in a while, for some reason, I get the insane notion to give it another try." Clearly, I need to find a way for my phone to have an alarm on it the next time I try. It should blast a siren and say, "Back away from the phone if you know what's good for you!" Or maybe it could just delete the apps anytime I attempt to download them. *Is that possible? Can AI do that these days?*

"What was so bad about the dates?"

"Let's see. One guy talked about his pet turtle the entire date and even showed me pictures. Another began the date with a list of dos and don'ts he found acceptable on a first date. It included things like: *Don't speak for the first ten minutes after the server brings the food, Don't order alcohol or dessert*—even though a prior rule stated I was paying my own way—*Don't order any seafood*, and oh yeah, this was my favorite, *Do compliment him on his manners.* Then there were the guys only looking for a hookup. One guy was literally on another date at the same time as ours. He wanted to see which one was more likely to end in sex."

I won't mention the guy who took one look at me and said it wasn't going to work out and left. Or the number of no-shows. They probably saw me and left, too, but didn't feel the need to say it to my face. *Which is worse?* I think I prefer the no-shows, even though they wasted more time because I sat waiting.

Brody's frown deepened with every example, and now he's staring at me like he's attempting to decipher a puzzle or mystery. It could be anything from *Why does she keep trying?* to *How can she be such a disaster?*

"What are you looking for in a guy?"

I blink at him. *Does he think my standards are too high? Did I sound whiny and complaining? Should I have been thankful for those dates as if any at all are good enough for me?*

"Seriously. It sounds like you need to filter out the deadbeats."

*Oh. That sounds better.* "I'm not sure the app does that. And people lie."

He shrugs. "Maybe online dating isn't the way to go. But you should know what you're looking for. Do you have White Knight Syndrome?"

I narrow my eyes at him. "If by that you mean *Am I waiting for a man to sweep me off my feet and solve all my problems for me?* Then no." Although in theory, the idea holds some appeal. I'm not delusional enough to think that fantasy exists in real life, however.

"Sorry. I didn't mean to offend you. I meant some women and men have this ideal partner in their head. They expect perfection."

"Perfection doesn't exist."

"I agree. So what do you want?"

*What do I want?* It's not like I ever sat down and compiled a list of the type of man I want to date. My options were always slim, so I had to keep my expectations low. It's probably why I stayed with Aaron for so long.

"I want a partner. I want to solve our problems together. I want a man who loves me and will put me first. We'll put each other first." *I won't be third or last on the list behind his work, hobbies, family, or friends.* "We'll work through any relationship issues together." *He won't run away at the first sign of trouble or blame everything on me.* "We'll compromise. It won't all be one-sided." *He'll care what I think and what*

*I want.* "We'll share some of the same interests." *I still need to figure out what my interests are, but they'll be similar.*

I turn and stare at Brody. "Does that sound unreasonable? Are my expectations too high?"

"No, you don't sound unreasonable. You absolutely should demand all those things and more." Brody cups my cheeks in his warm hands. His hazel eyes stare into mine before his lids close, and he presses his lips to mine.

My brain goes haywire. It doesn't know whether I should faint from shock or shout, "Hallelujah!" and kiss him back for all he's worth. My pulse thrums in my neck. Pleasure and nervousness battle so hard that I get a little lightheaded.

His lips continue to caress mine, like he's discovering how we fit.

If the way my body responds to him is any indication, I think we fit just fine.

He cradles my head and tilts it back as he deepens our kiss.

My hands flutter in my lap. I don't want to grab him and scare him off, but I ache to touch him.

His soft lips nuzzle against mine before he presses a lingering kiss on them. "You deserve to be cherished and loved, Mon. Don't let anyone give you less." He kisses my forehead softly and lets me go.

Then Brody gets up from the couch and walks into the guest room and closes the door.

*What just happened? Why did he kiss me? Better yet, why did he stop?*

# Chapter Seventeen

The sunset over the lake is spectacular. I always envy the view Kerry has here on the mountain.

Taking a sip of my dry white wine, I turn away from the wall of windows and join the book-club ladies milling around the kitchen island.

"I was a teacher at the high school during the time period we suspect the journal was written in, and I don't recollect anyone named Linny with a sister named Sassy. There were a few pregnancies, but I know all the families, and they just don't fit." Sally plants her hands on her hips and shakes her head. "Linny has to be one of the summer people or from another town."

*How could I have forgotten Sally was a high school teacher back then?* She was one of my high school teachers too. With everything going on in my mind and my life, it's a miracle I'm still functioning.

"I'm glad we have you for a source, Sally. I was trying to figure out how I could access the records without doing something illegal. I even chatted up some of the older teachers about any teenage pregnancies under the guise of a research paper a friend is doing." Kerry puts a scoop of dip and a handful of chips on her plate. "Wish I'd thought to ask you before I made up that elaborate story."

"Me too." Lucinda smacks her forehead with her palm. "I even talked to my dad about the possibility of subpoenaing records. I'm not licensed in New Hampshire, so I can't do it. I gave him a line about a fictitious client. Apparently, it's even harder to subpoena school records than I anticipated."

Franny laughs. "I never dreamed we'd all go to such lengths to discover who the author of the journal I found is, but I'm glad I'm not the only one mildly obsessed. I agree with Sally. Unless Linny vacationed here just that one summer, I'm thinking she's one of the summer set or she lives in a nearby town. Not sure why the journal was buried on our property. Mitch and I haven't found any evidence she stayed with the former owners of our house. We even called all the relatives still living. None of them recall a Linny."

Lucinda points a piece of celery at her sister. "Franny and I also checked everything available at the library and came up empty-handed."

"Ditto on the museum," Olivia says.

I wince. "I'm afraid I haven't had a chance to go to the newspaper and check back issues yet."

Tina waves her hand around while holding a chip. "No worries. I did, and I found no mention of any of the variations of names you came up with. Great call on that, by the way, Monica. I wouldn't have thought to check all the names Linny could be a nickname for."

"Yes, that text was helpful. I didn't think of it either. How did you come up with that list anyway? There were like a dozen names on it. Linda, Lynn, and Melinda all came to mind, but I would never have thought of Evelyn, Katlyn, Aislinn, or... I can't remember the others." Barbara pops a cherry tomato into her mouth.

I smile. "I borrowed Tina's baby name book she left at school in the teacher's room and went through it at lunchtime."

Tina laughs. "I forgot I left it at school."

Rebecca sighs. "So, we're all agreed we'll have to expand our search? No one uncovered anything centered on Granite Cove? Rachelle and I went to the town hall and came up empty too."

Aunt Aggie shakes her head while she chomps on a handful of nuts. "Police station was a bust too. No reports of stolen babies or kidnapping, so either Linny never reported it, or she didn't report it in Granite

Cove. Pretty sure Sally or I would've remembered something like that anyway. Missing babies get a lot of attention."

"I even tried to get information out of Dad about any lawyers who might've handled private adoptions." Lucinda wrinkles her nose. "He wasn't very helpful, but it's an avenue we need to address. Linny's parents took her baby. Where did it go?"

Kerry closes her fridge and says as she fills the charcuterie plate, "I had the same thought and did some research on the internet for any churches, hospitals, or other organizations that might've handled an adoption like that. Records are usually sealed. There is a public record where if all parties list themselves to be contacted, they can find one another. But since we're not any of the parties..."

"So let's reiterate what we do know. Her name is Linny, or that's her nickname. Her sister's name is Sassy or, again, nickname. Most likely didn't live in Granite Cove. She was sixteen and pregnant. And she had a baby boy before her asshole parents ripped him away from her." Rebecca takes a drink of her wine. "Did I forget anything?"

Franny fiddles with her necklace. "I think that sums it up."

"So why don't we keep our present assignments but expand the search to nearby towns?" Rachelle looks around the room. "Any objections?"

Olivia raises her hand. "I don't object to that, but we should also talk to all our families, at least the ones who lived in the area around that time, to compile a list of summer people who could've fit."

Rebecca aims a finger at them both. "Excellent points, ladies. I don't have family from that time, but my husband certainly does."

I sip my wine while the ladies discuss who might have information. I could talk to my parents, but they'll want to know why I'm asking. I suppose I could just explain the journal. They've both been rather silent since the total fiasco with Brian's future in-laws. I told Katy's mother I would handle the payments and any future issues, and she wasn't to disturb my parents again. She was less than pleasant until she heard the money she demanded would be forthcoming, then she was as sweet as pie. *Deceptively so, like she's hiding a nasty surprise beneath the crust, like mold.*

"Monica?" Kerry appears at my shoulder. "Everything okay? You're not still worried about Lisette, are you? Has she given you any more problems?"

I shake my head. "She hasn't spoken a word to me. I'm not sure if that's a good or bad sign." She could lie in wait or prepare an attack. She's like a sneaky predator that way—like an eel hiding in a cave or a lion stalking its prey on the savannah.

"Then why are you so quiet? You seem distracted."

*Oh, nothing. My former crush has not only returned to town, he's also now living with me, and yesterday, he kissed me, and I've avoided him since because I'm worried it was a pity kiss.*

"Monica?"

I could really use a second opinion. It's not like my plan of avoidance can continue to work. "What would you think if a guy... a friend of sorts... Well, if he kissed you after you kind of complained about all the bad dates you'd had in the past? Would you think it was a pity kiss to make you feel better?"

Kerry eyes widen, and her jaw drops.

*I should've kept my mouth shut.*

"What kind of kiss?"

"Why on earth would you assume it was a pity kiss?"

"What guy? Do we know him?"

My gaze shoots around the room. The ladies are all staring at me and clearly heard what I said to Kerry. I don't even know who asked what. My face is probably as red as a tomato. Even my chest is hot.

Kerry touches my arm. "Why do you think that?"

Olivia hugs me. "Monica, you're a beautiful, smart, accomplished woman. If a guy kissed you, it had nothing to do with pity."

"Amen."

"Absolutely."

The ladies are all vigorously nodding and have formed a circle around me.

"You don't understand. He caught me setting up a dating profile, which was embarrassing enough, but then I spewed out all this babble about the bad dates I've been on. I think he felt sorry for me."

Rebecca crosses her arms. "What kind of kiss are we talking about?

A peck on the cheek? A kiss on the forehead? On the lips? With or without tongue?"

"On the lips. No tongue."

"Was it more than a peck?" Lucinda asks.

I nod.

Rebecca snorts. "It wasn't a pity kiss."

Several of the ladies shake their heads.

"Young lady, do we need to have an intervention? Men don't go around giving pity kisses. Are you interested in him or not? Is he getting too handsy and you want to keep him in the friend zone?" Aunt Aggie stares at me with her hands on her hips and a frown on her face. She looks like she's ready to do battle.

The image of her interrogating Brody makes me nauseous. I can never let her know who I'm talking about. "I'm interested."

She grins. "Okay, then. That's a different story."

"Monica, I agree with Aggie. Guys don't think like we do. They don't kiss a woman unless they're attracted to them. It wasn't a pity kiss." Rebecca tops off my wine. "Now, do we know this guy? Is he good enough for you?"

I smile at her. "You don't know him." Aunt Aggie is the only one who might make the connection if she hears his name, and I'm not ready for everyone to know about Brody yet. I haven't wrapped my head around my feelings or the thought that he might be interested in me. I'm still having a hard time believing it wasn't a pity kiss, no matter what the ladies say. They're my friends. They might only be being kind to avoid hurting my feelings.

Franny slides between Olivia and Kerry. "Monica, can I talk to you a minute?"

"Sure." I glance at everyone as they turn back to the island to give us privacy.

She leads me over to the windows. "You can tell me to mind my own business, but as your friend, I would just like to say I really struggled with insecurities, especially with Mitch. I couldn't believe he could actually be interested in me, let alone love me. I get the feeling you might be struggling a little too."

I close my eyes and let out a shaky breath. "He's so far out of my league."

Franny shakes her head. "Oh no, he's not. I don't even know who you're talking about, but I guarantee you he is not out of your league."

"He's gorgeous. On a scale of one to ten, he'd break the scale. I'm a solid five on my best day."

She sucks in a breath. "That is absolutely not true. Trust me on this. I thought the same thing about myself. You are beautiful. You need to see that when you look in the mirror and believe it. It took me time, but I've come to believe Mitch when he tells me I'm beautiful. And even more importantly, I'm able to see my own beauty too." She nibbles on her lip and plays with her necklace. "I'm not sure what caused your insecurities. For me, I grew up with a great deal of criticism. You've heard some of the stories of my mother. I had to learn that what others said about me didn't define me. Only I can define me."

"And what if I feel unworthy because of me and not because of anyone else?" I whisper.

Franny wraps her arms around me and whispers into my ear, "You are worthy, Monica. I promise you. You are worthy of love and all the wonderful things that go with it."

"You don't know me, not really. There are things in my past..."

"I may not know your past, but I know you now. You were the very first one to offer me friendship. You opened my eyes to the people and possibilities around me I was too blind to see. If you hadn't persisted in inviting me to book club..." Tears fill her eyes. "My friendships with you and all the ladies mean the world to me."

I give her a wobbly smile. "Book club has meant everything to me too."

"Monica, honey, is this about the anniversary of Rosie's death? I understand it's a hard time of year for you and your folks. I talked to your mom, and I thought she was handling it well this year, but I know she hides her feelings sometimes. Is it a bad one?" Aunt Aggie rubs my back.

Franny stares at me with a perplexed expression stamped on her face. I don't talk about Rosie to anyone. Brody is the first in a very long time.

Aunt Aggie's worried look turns to stricken as she watches me. It must be dawning on her that no one here knows about Rosie.

I smile to reassure her. "It's always hard, but Mom and Dad seem to be doing okay." I glance at Franny. "Rosie is... was my sister. My twin. She died twenty years ago in a car accident."

"Oh, Monica, I'm so sorry. I had no idea." Franny hugs me tightly.

"That's because we don't... I don't talk about her to anyone. At first, I think it was because it was too hard on my parents. They couldn't bring themselves to talk about her, and I didn't want to upset them. Then it was because everyone would whisper or give me pitying looks if they knew. I also carried around a lot of guilt because I blamed myself for the accident."

Aunt Aggie sucks in a harsh breath. "Honey, why would you blame yourself? It was a car accident. You were a child."

My hand shakes so much that Franny takes the wineglass out of my hand and sets it on a nearby table.

"Because I pretended to be sick so I could stay home. Mom had to ask the Swifts to drive Rosie to gymnastics."

I'm crushed in Aunt Aggie's grip. She snivels in my ear. "You aren't to blame. No one was but especially not you."

"I'm trying to accept that." Maybe if I hear it enough times, I'll start to believe it.

Tissues appear in my peripheral vision as Aunt Aggie releases me.

Franny rubs my arm. "Why don't we go sit down."

I follow Franny to the couch. The ladies fill the remainder of the seating, giving me sympathetic looks and sad smiles. But it doesn't fill me with dread or make me want to run and hide anymore. *Why? Because I know they only have my best interests at heart? Have I finally reached another stage in the grieving process?*

Aunt Aggie sits next to me and grips my hand. "I should've intervened a long time ago."

I frown at her. *What is she talking about?*

"You always take on too much. You've become more of a parent to your parents than they are to you."

I shake my head. "Aunt Aggie—"

"Let me finish. You've always been so responsible. Practically raised your little brother. I should've seen it was because you were trying to compensate for losing your sister. I should've known you were hurting. I failed you." She sobs into her hand.

"No. Please stop. Aunt Aggie, don't you know you and Uncle Dennis's visits were some of the few times I felt like a kid? You always made them fun. You couldn't have known how I felt. I never told anyone. I was too scared. You know how fragile Mom is. And Dad... He had enough to deal with too. I guess to some degree, I was trying to make up for Rosie's loss—which I blamed myself for. And I never felt like I measured up. But none of that is on you. You're a part of some of my fondest memories growing up."

I glance around the room. "I'm so sorry. I've made this book-club meeting all about me instead of the journal."

Gasps and denials fill the room.

Lucinda scoots to the end of her seat across from me. "Monica, you're our friend. You're always here for all of us. Let us be here for you."

"I second that. What are friends for if not to tell you when you're being ridiculous?"

I stare at Rebecca as a few of the ladies give her a wide-eyed stare like they can't believe she called me ridiculous.

"Don't give me that look. Remember when I thought I had to do everything myself with my brother?"

Rachelle snorts. "Pot and kettle."

Rebecca gives her sister a glare. "My point is I didn't tell any of you about my brother or what I was going through because I thought they were my issues to deal with."

"And you're a control freak. Who I love dearly." Rachelle blows her sister a kiss.

Rebecca sticks her tongue out at her sister then turns back to me. "I admit I am. It's a coping mechanism. When tragedy strikes, we tend to want to control everything around us so it doesn't happen again. Which is why I recognize you doing the same thing I did. I blamed myself too. My parents' deaths weren't my fault any more than your sister's was yours. Shit happens. Terrible, awful shit. But it happens despite what we do or don't do. All we can do is keep living."

# Chapter Eighteen

I shut off my headlights before I turn into my driveway. *Coward!* I'm too emotional to handle seeing Brody right now. It took a lot out of me to be a blubbering, crying mess as my friends all sympathy cried with me. *Freeing too.*

My motion detector lights come on as I walk up the path, and I freeze. *Nice going, Monica. Forgot about your own lights on your own house.* I sigh and walk up to the door. It's late enough that he might've gone to bed already. I didn't see any lights on in the living room, and I don't hear anything inside. He might not even be home.

*Did he leave without saying goodbye? Is his parents' house fixed already?* Maybe he's on a date. A solid mass of pain grips my chest. *Please don't let him be on a date.*

*Use your brain Monica, Brody's Jeep is in the driveway.* Unless someone picked him up, he's here.

*Oh lord, what if he brought her here? He wouldn't do that, would he?* If I have to witness him with another woman, I will legit throw up.

I close my eyes. *I am in so deep already.*

*Suck it up, Monica.* I'm going to have to face him sooner or later.

*Later would be good.*

I unlock the front door and ease inside. The door to the guest room is open, but there isn't a light on. I can't see if the bathroom door is closed or if there's a light on in there. Dropping my tote to the ground, I sigh. *Sneaking into my own house might be a new low for me.*

The light on the end table switches on. Brody sits in the armchair in the corner, watching me.

*Is spontaneous paralysis a thing?* I feel like my lungs might've atrophied in my chest.

"Do you want me to leave?"

I blink at him as I try to process his words. "Why would I want you to leave?"

"You leave before I get up in the morning. An hour earlier than normal. You don't come home until late. Either you're avoiding me because I'm imposing on you, you're freaked out about the kiss the other night, or..." He shrugs. "Just tell me."

"The second one."

He looks away. "Okay."

"I'm sorry. I panicked. I've been avoiding you because I didn't know what to do."

"This is your house, Mon. You don't have to tiptoe around me. I'll get my things and move out." He stands.

"What? Why? Where are you going to go?"

"Don't worry about it." He walks across the room.

"Brody, you don't have to leave." *Why does he think he has to leave? Because I'm a child who doesn't know how to react to an innocent kiss.*

"I make you so uncomfortable that you feel you have to hide from me and avoid your own house. I'm not going to keep doing that to you. Where even were you? I was worried. Please tell me you weren't sitting in your car somewhere."

"That's not—no. I had plans. Brody..."

"Were you on a date?" He turns away. "Never mind. That was none of my business."

I follow him down the hall to the guest room. "You think I was on a date?" I glance down at my pants and blouse. "Dressed in my work clothes?"

He flicks on the light and glances over his shoulder. A scowl takes over his expression. "Have you been crying?" He rubs his hands over his face. "Were you crying because of me?"

"What? No." *What is happening right now? Is he upset because he thinks I overreacted to the kiss?*

He puts his hands in the front pockets of his jeans. "Then why? Was it Rosie? Or did someone say something to upset you?"

I lift my hands and drop them to my sides. "It was partly about Rosie. I finally told my friends about her, or my aunt did, then it all came out about blaming myself, and we were all pretty much crying by the end."

"So you were out with friends?"

I bite my lip and nod. "I should've texted you. I shouldn't have avoided you. I'm sorry. I'm not used to people worrying about my whereabouts. I don't want you to go. Wait until your parents' house is fixed. Please."

He stares out the window as if he can see beyond the dim reflection of the room. "I don't think that's a good idea."

I wrap my arms around my waist. "Can I ask why?" *Was the kiss meaningless to him, or was my reaction the problem? Did he decide I'm too much work, or did he not like the kiss?*

"Brody, why did you ask if I was on a date?"

He glances at me then looks away. "You were making a dating profile. It's a logical assumption that it would lead to dates."

"It would if I ever finished it."

"You didn't finish it?"

"No. It was momentary insanity. Or desperation. Pick one. Online dating isn't for me. I, ah, kind of wondered if you were on a date when I saw the house was dark. I was afraid I was going to walk in on something." *More like sick to my stomach.*

He studies me. "You thought I was on a date? That I would bring a woman here?"

I shrug. "We never discussed any rules about dating or bringing someone home."

He rubs his face. "I can't decide whether you're worried I'll bring someone or if you're trying to tell me you might be the one to bring a date home. If it's the latter, I definitely need to move out because there's no way in hell I'm going to watch you bring another guy here."

"I don't want to date anyone else, Brody. And I really, really don't want to watch you date someone else."

A smile spreads across his face. "You don't?"

I return his smile. "No, I don't."

He steps toward me. "So when you said you were avoiding me because of the kiss, it wasn't because you didn't want me to kiss you again?"

"No, it was because I thought you kissed me because you felt sorry for me." *How's that for a truth bomb?*

He cups my face in his palms and leans his forehead against mine. "I don't understand how your mind works."

I laugh. "Join the club."

He chuckles and brushes my lips with his. "For the record, I kissed you because you're a desirable woman who I can't stop thinking about."

"Oh." My heart feels like it's taking flight out of my chest.

Brody kisses me then wraps his arms around me, and I slide my hands over his chest.

His tongue touches mine, and a zing of heat and pleasure goes straight to my core.

*Brody is kissing me! Why do I suddenly feel like a teenager receiving her first kiss?* No, that's not right because none of my teenage kisses ever came close to this.

One of his hands settles at my waist while the other presses between my shoulder blades, pulling me into his chest. I slide my hands around his neck as he deepens the kiss.

Warmth spreads over me like I'm lying on the beach beneath the summer sun.

Need curls through me—need for more. More of Brody. More of this pleasure.

Brody turns his head to the side. His warm breath puffs against my cheek. "We need to slow down."

*We do?*

He leans his forehead against mine. "I don't want to mess this up.

You're too important to me, Mon. We need to make sure we're both on the same page with this. I want you to be sure."

Oh, right. He's only here for the summer.

*Am I okay with a fling?*

He's Brian's best friend. I'm bound to run into him again after the summer. *How will I feel seeing him after this is over? How will I feel if he's moved on to someone new and I'm still pining over him?*

*Will it hurt more or less having him for a short time and letting him go?*

"And your silence right there is why we need to slow down. You need to figure out if this is really what you want."

"I..."

"It's okay." His hands rest loosely on my hips. "I'm not going anywhere until you tell me to. Take as long as you need to be sure."

I bite my lip. *Why does what he's saying make sense? Why can't we just deal with the consequences later?*

He kisses me softly, and I want to groan in frustration.

"Get some sleep. We'll talk later when we both have clear heads."

"I don't know if it's terrifying or a good thing that you're the logical and responsible one suddenly."

He chuckles and kisses me again before letting me go. "I have my moments. Good night, Monica. Sweet dreams."

*Yeah, right.* It'll be a miracle if I can sleep after this. I'd take care of my needs myself if I weren't terrified he'd hear.

*Wait, what if he did?* Maybe he would change his mind about waiting. I lean against my closed bedroom door. But then we'd be past the point of no return. As much as I hate admitting it, Brody is right. I need to be sure I can handle a summer fling with him.

# Chapter Nineteen

Katy's mom stares at me from across the table with an expression on her face like she ate something unpleasant, except we haven't even ordered any food yet. *Why did I get stuck sitting across from the woman?* Oh yes, I'm trying to shield my parents from their toxic behavior, so I took one for the team. I suppose it could be worse, and I could be sitting next to her. Instead, her husband and daughter flank her. Brian sits at the head of the table, on Katy's left. As soon as Mom sat next to Brian, I took the seat next to her, forcing Dad to sit on my other side so my parents wouldn't be directly across from Katy's mom. Technically, Dad and Mom are next to and across from Katy's dad, but he's usually the lesser of two evils. My father and brother both gave me weird looks, but they refrained from commenting.

Why Katy and Brian thought this dinner was a good idea is beyond me. My parents did not want to go but also didn't want to disappoint Brian. When they arrived, Dad whispered to me, asking if I took care of everything like I promised. From his tone, I can guess he thought I used reasoning with Katy's parents rather than telling them I would pay my parents' share of the wedding and that they were to deal with only me from now on. He wouldn't be happy, but Katy's parents aren't the type to be reasoned with. They only see their selfish interests.

The water has a chemical taste, and I briefly consider spitting it back into the glass. But I lower the glass to the table and try to wipe the grimace off my face. A pinched whistling jolts me in my seat. I keep my gaze on the table in front of me because I know the source. Katy's mom makes strange random noises out of her nose. I have no idea why, and it does seem involuntary, but it's disconcerting. It probably wouldn't bother me in the least if she weren't so unpleasant.

A sharp kick hits me in the shin. I frown and glance at Brian, but even his legs aren't that long, and he's talking to Katy. I don't bother turning to Mom on my left because it's physically impossible for her to manage a kick like that to my right leg. I look across the table at the woman who is fast becoming enemy number one in my book. *How pointy are her shoes anyway? Witch shoes for a witch. How would she feel if I kicked her back?*

Katy's mom glares at me. "We need to discuss payment terms. I want written proof you are paying half the reception fees. I've added a few close friends to the invite list, and we've extended the open-bar selections."

*Succotash! Succotash! Succotash!* Stiffening in my seat, I imagine throwing my water into her face. I resist the urge to glance right or left to check whether Brian or my parents heard her. I don't want to call attention to the conversation if by some miracle they didn't. *What does this woman not understand about keeping Brian and my parents out of it? Is she that dense or that malicious?*

*And where the heck does she get off extending the invite list when my family has been denied even our closest relatives, let alone any friends?*

*She wants written proof? Like I can't afford to pay it? Well, I can't, but I'm figuring it out.* I said I would, and I will. *Hateful woman.*

"What's she talking about, Monica?" Brian's voice rumbles on my right.

My parents lean forward and look down the table.

Deborah—*better known as harpy from hell on my evildoer list for eternity*—raises her chin haughtily and says to Brian, "Your sister told me I am not permitted to speak to your parents about the wedding and that all future conversations are to go through her. She also claims to be the one paying their portion, but I have doubts about her ability on a teacher's salary."

My mother sucks in a breath beside me.

My father clenches his fists on the table on either side of his plate.

"If you hadn't ambushed and attacked my parents in the first place, I wouldn't have had to interfere. And I very clearly told you to keep it between us so Brian and Katy wouldn't be dragged into your ridiculous demands, antagonistic attitude, hateful criticisms, and downright-appalling behavior. But even that was beyond your capabilities."

"Do you see what you're marrying into?" Deborah sneers at her daughter. "Brian, I insist you put your sister in her place. I will not be spoken to or treated in this manner."

Brian ignores her and continues to stare at me. "She ambushed Mom and Dad?" He looks past me at our parents.

Mom bows her head and sniffles.

"She came to our house and accused us of not caring enough about you and taking financial advantage of them." Dad points at Katy's parents. "Demanded we pay more than what we had already agreed to. Monica came over after and said she would handle it. I never dreamed she meant she would pay in our stead." I feel Dad's stare. "What were you thinking, honey?"

Brian shoves his chair back and stands. "She was doing what she always does—trying to fix everything. Monica, I'm a grown-ass man. I don't need you to fix everything anymore. You should have come to me."

"I'm sorry. You're right. I was trying to help, but you're an adult, and they're your future in-laws to deal with." *Wish I'd never tried to keep the peace. I should've told the old bat to go straight to hell.*

Deborah hisses out a breath. "You are impossible."

"Enough!" Brian points at her. "My sister helped raise me. She has always been there for me, no matter what. The fact that she was willing to pay for our wedding, which I can only imagine how she would've managed, is telling enough. You had no right to attack my parents. They agreed to an amount they could afford and said it was the best they could do. You're the one who keeps adding to the damn invite list and expanding the wedding plans. I'm sick of the whole mess. My family

isn't paying a damn dime because there's not going to be a wedding."
Brian stalks away.

Horrified, Katy leaps up with a gasp and chases him.

Deborah gapes after them like a fish out of water.

*Would a slow clap be remiss?*

Dad stands. "Let's go, Penelope. Monica, I'll talk to you later."

*Great.* I watch my parents gather their things and walk away, then I stand and pick up my purse. Katy's father has an irritated scowl on his face. He doesn't talk much, and I assumed it was because his wife never shuts up and he lets her do what she wants. I have no idea what their marriage dynamic is, and I really don't care. Deborah glares at me like everything is my fault and she wishes I would burst into flames on the spot.

"You accused my parents of not caring about their son and not wanting Brian and Katy to get married because they said they couldn't afford more money than they already promised. You're a hypocrite of the worst kind. You're the one who doesn't care. Because if you did, you would never have acted so selfishly and cruelly. This is Brian's and Katy's wedding, not yours—at least it was. It's not about you. It's about them. It honestly amazes me that Katy comes from the two of you. Goodbye, and I sincerely hope I never have the misfortune to speak to either one of you ever again."

I walk away with my head held high. My little brother made me very proud tonight. He not only stood up for himself and his family, but he also put a bully in her place. I hope he and Katy can figure out how to move forward.

The waitress heads my way. I briefly consider stopping her and paying for the drinks we ordered but hadn't received yet, but the Lewises are still at the table. They made the reservation and all the problems. They can pay for the dang drinks, even though I'm sure they'll say we're taking financial advantage of them once again. *Karma sometimes does work.*

# Chapter Twenty

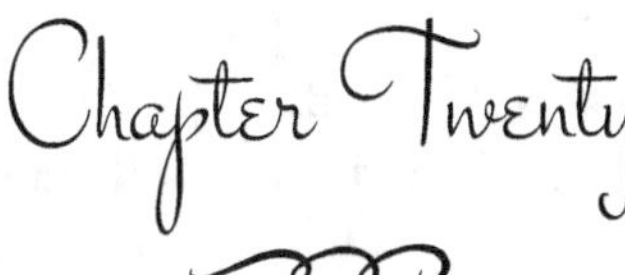

"Hey, how was dinner?" Brody waits for me in the living room. He glances at his phone. "You're early, aren't you? Not that I'm complaining." He smiles and walks toward me.

Giddiness washes over me at the sight of him. He made me breakfast this morning and kissed me goodbye at the door. Just a peck, really, but it sent me off to work on a high. I'm both grateful and a little disappointed he hasn't pushed for a decision on a summer fling. If he did push, I'd probably say yes without thinking it through, which is probably why he's not pushing.

"You won't believe what happened. It was both a train wreck and a cause for celebration."

He puts his hands on my hips as he kisses me. "Tell me all about it. You mind if I grab something to eat while you do? I haven't had dinner yet."

"Neither have I, actually. We didn't get that far before Brian stormed out."

Brody pauses on his way to the kitchen. "He okay?"

"I think so. I'm actually proud of him for standing up for himself and us. Is that wrong?"

"Why would it be wrong, and why did he have to stand up and

against whom? Did someone insult you or your family?" Anger contorts his face.

"Not to rehash the complete debacle, but Katy's parents are a nightmare. They've always been difficult to get along with, but where money is involved, they're very offensive and, frankly, selfish. They've made all the wedding arrangements, monopolized the invite list, yet still demanded my parents pay for half. My parents agreed to the initial amount, and they made it clear that was all they could pay." I rest my hands on the back of one of the chairs at the table. "Fast forward a few weeks, and Deborah, Katy's mother, showed up at my parents' house and verbally attacked them. She accused them of taking financial advantage of her and her husband, claimed they did so much more for Brian and Katy than my parents, and accused them of not caring enough about Brian or the wedding. There's more, but for brevity's sake, that's enough. Of course, my parents were really upset. I promised them I would handle Katy's parents and the situation. As much as I wanted to tell Deborah and her husband where they could go, I decided to try to keep the peace and promised to pay for it myself as long as she didn't approach my parents again. Well, before we even ordered dinner, the woman kicked me under the table then demanded I put my promise to pay in writing. Brian and my parents overheard, of course, because she wasn't discreet, then chaos ensued. He put her in her place, chastised me for not telling him and treating him like a kid, declared the wedding was off, and stormed out of the restaurant. I texted him, but he hasn't replied. You haven't heard from him, have you?"

Brody shakes his head. "Why didn't you tell me this was going on? I could've helped you."

I smile. "That's sweet of you, but I'm not in the habit of airing my family's dirty laundry."

He crosses his arms. "Translation: you're not in the habit of asking for help."

I sigh. "Accurate."

"Have a seat. I'll get us something to eat, then we can track down Brian together and get this all sorted out."

I do as he says while he rummages in the fridge. *Do I really need to think about the pros and cons of having a summer fling with Brody? My* former crush is standing in my kitchen, making me dinner. He's gorgeous, considerate, kind, helpful, and for some insane reason, he's attracted to me.

The risk is getting a broken heart when the summer is over.

But if I protect my heart and turn down the chance to be with Brody even for a short time, I might regret it and always wonder what it could've been like.

He glances over his shoulder. "I hope you like quesadillas. They're quick, and we have all the ingredients."

"Sounds perfect to me."

He winks and stacks ingredients by the stove.

*A few months of this? Yes, please.*

Of course, if Katy isn't able to change Brian's mind about the wedding, Brody could change his mind about staying for the summer. He's only in Granite Cove for the wedding.

"What did Katy do when Brian called the wedding off and left?"

"She ran out after him. My parents followed, warning me we would talk later, which means I can expect a lecture from them. I said a few more words to Katy's parents, then I left too."

He grins at me over his shoulder. "A few more words, huh?"

"Don't judge me too harshly. They're awful people."

"I'm not judging you, Mon. I love the way you love your family and do everything you can for them. People like Katy's parents will never understand that. Trust me. I'm well acquainted with their kind."

*Does he mean his parents?* "You want to talk about it?"

"Some other time." He carries two plates over with slices of quesadilla oozing melted cheese with salsa and sour cream on top.

The warm, cheesy goodness melts in my mouth. "This is so good. Seriously, where did you learn to cook? And don't give me some vague answer like before."

"I was a cook in a diner for a while."

I stop mid-chew. *Brody worked in a diner... as a cook?* I can't picture it. Wait, I can. He wears a tight white T-shirt and faded jeans covered by a white apron. *Hmm...*

"My parents disowned me, remember? Had to support myself somehow while I tried to make music work as a living."

"Well, I, for one, am very thankful I get to benefit from your resourcefulness." I take another bite while he smiles at me.

*Sigh. That dimple gets me every time.*

"Brody?"

He glances up from his plate.

"If we do this…" I point at him then me. "Could we keep it between ourselves?" So there are no witnesses to my broken heart when you go. "My family is going through a lot right now, and I don't want to complicate things."

He puts down his fork. "Probably for the best, considering."

*Does he mean the wedding drama or the fact that he's leaving at the end of the summer?*

It doesn't matter. The result is still the same.

"Do you want to discuss it now?"

I set down my fork as well. "Sure. What do you want to discuss?"

"I want to make sure that you had time to think it over. There's no rush. We have time."

"Brody, if you've changed your mind, just tell me." *You might as well stab me in the chest, but I can take it. I'm used to pain.*

He stands and walks around the table. "I haven't changed my mind." He pulls me out of the chair and into his arms. He rests his hands on the small of my back. "Let's establish the rules."

*There are rules?*

"Like what?" I'm good with rules. I'm a perfect example of a rule follower. This is probably where he'll warn me not to get attached or fall in love with him.

"Like, we're exclusive. You delete all dating apps and profiles. No dates except with me."

"I can do that as long as the rule applies to us both." He doesn't need to know I already deleted them again.

He kisses me softly. "It does. You already said it stays between us, so that's rule number two." He kisses me again.

"Is there a rule number three?" My lips brush his.

"Just be honest. Don't leave me guessing about what's going through your pretty head."

"Hmm. And are you going to be honest with me too?"

"Yes. This only works if we're up front with each other."

"Agreed."

Smiling, he deepens the kiss. I grip his shoulders and melt against his chest.

This might be the best decision I've ever made. And if we end up where I'm hoping tonight, it just might be the best day too.

Someone knocks on the door.

Brody and I freeze against each other. I drop my head to his shoulder and groan. *Just my luck.*

"Odds are that's Brian," Brody whispers into my ear.

"I know." I glance at the table holding our half-eaten dinner and the door. *How am I going to explain this to Brian?*

Can I clear the table while Brody hides in the guest room?

Another knock sounds.

"Go answer the door."

"But..." I glance at him, the table, and the door.

"He's already noticed my Jeep in your driveway, Mon. So get any ideas of stuffing me into a closet out of your head. I'm just here to pick up my dog, who you so kindly watched for me."

"Oh, good call." I paste a smile on my face and answer the door.

Brian looks at me then over my head. "Brody."

"He's here to pick up Hank."

Brian frowns as he walks in, and I close the door. "Who's Hank? You got a new boyfriend I don't know about? Just how many secrets are you keeping from me?"

I open and close my mouth a few times. *Ouch.*

*Wait a minute. How does he not know who Hank is?*

"Hank's my dog. Monica watched him while I was out of town."

On cue, Hank waddles out into the living room. It's a toss-up of whose bed he was sleeping in until now.

"When did you get a dog?" Brian bends over and pets Hank. "Hey, fella."

"It's a relatively recent development. How are you, man? Monica filled me in some."

Brian sighs and says to me, "Yeah, you and I need to have a talk."

"Need me to take off?" Brody takes Hank's leash off the hook by the door.

Brian shakes his head. "No, you can stay. That talk between me and my sister can wait. You being here actually saves me some time."

"The wedding back on?" I knew once he cooled down he'd change his mind. He loves Katy. It's a shame she has terrible parents. And it sucks that I'm going to have to endure their presence after all at a wedding.

"No."

*No?* Oh lord, please tell me he didn't break up with Katy because of her parents.

"Katy and I are eloping. And I want the two of you there with me."

# Chapter Twenty-One

"We're going to Las Vegas tonight and getting married tomorrow. Katy checked online, and we can get the marriage license and get married all in one day."

I'm completely speechless as I stare at Brian. *Las Vegas?* I thought he meant the town hall or something. Of course I want to support him and be there for him. *But Las Vegas?* "Brian, have you and Katy really thought this through? Are you sure you're not being impulsive?"

His smile disappears. "Yes, Katy and I want to get married."

"I know that. I meant about going to Las Vegas."

"Katy and I had a long talk. All the wedding planning has been getting to both of us. I thought she wanted the whole wedding shebang, so I didn't say anything about how overwhelming it was getting. And I knew it was taking a toll on Mom and Dad. But I didn't know how much. And I had no idea what you were sacrificing either." He rolls his shoulders and cracks his neck. "It's all too much. When I told Katy how I felt, she was relieved. She'd been feeling the same way because her parents were on her back every damn day about the wedding and our family's role in it. I had no idea what she was going through. Going to Las Vegas is exciting, and it still makes the occasion special. Getting married at the town hall doesn't hold the same appeal."

It's hard to argue with all that.

"I know asking the two of you to fly to Las Vegas for the weekend at the last minute is a lot, so it's okay if you can't swing it."

I hug my brother. "If this is what you really want, of course I'm going. I wouldn't miss it. I can't speak for Brody, of course."

Brian squeezes the breath out of me. "Love you, sis."

"I love you too." I smack his arm. "I guess I have some packing to do and arrangements to make."

Brian looks over his shoulder at Brody. "You in?"

An adorable grin spreads over Brody's face. "Just try to keep me away." He rubs his hands together. "Let's get this wedding weekend started."

Brian laughs. "There's an overnight flight out of Boston. Katy and I are already booked." He looks at his watch. "We have to leave in about an hour if we're going to make it on time."

Brody claps Brian on the back. "You head out and get your fiancée to the airport. I'll help your sister and make sure she gets to Vegas."

"Thanks, man." Brian hugs Brody then me again and grins. "Things happen for a reason, right?"

*Sometimes they do but not always.*

After Brian leaves, Brody rubs my arms. "You okay?"

"Yeah, just a little shocked." *Or a lot.* "Oh lord, there's so much to do. We need to book a flight, get hotel rooms, pack... Do we need a rental car? I've never been to Vegas. Have you? I have no idea what to expect except lights and people—lots of people."

"Breathe." Brody hugs me. "Yes, I've been to Vegas, and no we don't need a rental. I'll handle the hotel and flights while you pack a bag, okay?"

"Okay, if you're sure."

"I'm sure." He kisses me on my forehead. "Pack light. We can always pick up anything you need there."

*What the heck am I going to pack for Vegas?* My wardrobe consists of teacher-appropriate clothes, nothing for a place nicknamed Sin City.

Suddenly remembering, I stop in the hallway and spin around. "What about Hank?"

Brody looks up from his phone. "Got it covered. Don't worry."

I have a small suitcase. It should be big enough for a weekend trip. Now if I can just remember where I put it. I nibble on my lip. It's probably in the guest room closet.

"Need some help?" Brody comes up behind me while I'm digging in there.

I lower my arms from the top shelf. "See that suitcase behind those boxes? I need it."

His gaze shifts from the suitcase to me. "When's the last time you used it?"

"I don't remember. It's been a while." Traveling has always been in the back of my mind for some future day when everything calms down and I have the time and money. "Oh, Kelly's wedding in Texas."

That was a fun time. Kelly and Holden said their vows under a tree on a hill overlooking Holden's ranch. It was a small wedding but beautiful. Kelly was already a few months pregnant, but she barely showed. I went through two entire packages of tissues listening to the two of them recite their vows, and they included Trevor in them, too, because his official adoption went through. *Would I have become a mother to Trevor as seamlessly as Kelly?* I'd like to believe I have the capacity to love like that, but I guess you can never really know until it happens to you. And Kelly formed a strong bond with Holden's son the first day they met.

Brody moves the boxes and sets the suitcase down in front of me. "Do you not like to travel? Afraid of flying?"

"No, I just don't have many opportunities. I'd like to see the world someday."

He cups my cheek and rubs his thumb over my skin. "Maybe it's time to put yourself and your wants and needs first for a change."

*That's exactly what I'm doing by having this summer fling with you. If it ever gets started.* "Working on it."

He kisses me then swats me on my butt. "You'd better get packing. I booked us on the same flight as Brian out of Boston." He walks over and grabs his duffel from under the bed. "And don't worry. I booked us separate rooms at the hotel."

*Who was worried?*

"We can finish discussing those rules of ours when we get back." He winks and unzips his duffel.

*I guess Vegas isn't going to be as fun as I was beginning to hope.*

When I'm back in my bedroom, I sigh as I dump my suitcase on my bed and open my closet to stare at the contents. *Nope, still my boring old clothes. Nothing sexy or fun in here.*

At least Brody is still planning on our summer fling, even if it's delayed until we get back to Granite Cove. With the wedding no longer happening, he could've decided not to stay for the summer. *He still might.*

I slide clothes to the side, hoping something suitable is hiding between my black, gray, and navy clothes.

Brody is right. It's not like we can start our romance right under Brian's nose. I was the one who requested we keep it under wraps. Sharing a hotel room would've been a dead giveaway. *Nice going, Monica. You're sabotaging your own chance of happiness. No surprise there.*

Just for a moment, I imagine what it would be like if Brody and I were jetting off for a vacation, just the two of us, as a couple.

I pick a pair of black slacks and a gold blouse I wore for New Year's Eve once. The summer dress I find next isn't too shabby. It could pass for a wedding in Vegas.

School is out in less than two weeks. There's a chance Brody and I could get away for a weekend somewhere where no one would interrupt us.

Brody pokes his head in my closet. "I'm going to go take Hank to the kennel. I'll be back to pick you up in about half an hour, okay?"

"Oh, okay. Let me say goodbye to him." Hank is standing in the doorway to my room, watching us. "Do you think he knows he's going to the k-e-n-n-e-l? Will he be all right there? What do you know about this place?"

Brody kisses my temple when I stand up after petting Hank. "You're adorable. It's where I got him in the first place, and they're great."

"You got him here in Granite Cove?" No wonder Brian didn't know Brody had a dog.

"Yes. Gotta go if we're going to make the flight."

Right. I'll just rummage through my closet some more. *Succotash! I need to pack toiletries too.* I glance at my watch. Thirty minutes to pack, change into something comfortable for the overnight flight, and lock up my house for the weekend. *Yeah, no problem.*

By the time I hear Brody's Jeep in my driveway, I've changed into leggings, a T-shirt, and a sweatshirt, packed for the weekend, shut off lights, and unplugged any small appliances just to be safe. *Women could rule the world and make it a better place.*

I swing open the door with a smile on my face. Brody, Brian, and Katy are all walking up my front walk. *Aren't they supposed to be on their way to the airport already? Did they change their mind?*

"I picked them up on the way. Doesn't make any sense for us to take two cars when we're going on the same flight."

"Good thinking." I smile at Brody then Brian and Katy. "Who's ready to get married?"

Katy bounces on her toes and squeals in happiness. Brian hugs her.

Once we're all loaded up and on the way, Brody glances in the rearview mirror and asks, "Katy, are any of your friends joining us? I didn't think to ask before now." He frowns. "Not that they'd fit in my Jeep."

"Um, no. I don't really have any close-enough friends to ask to do this."

I turn in my seat. "What about your bridesmaids?" She and her mother discussed bridesmaids' dresses, so I know she was planning to have them.

"My mother made me ask the daughter of one of her friends and my cousin. I'm not that close to either of them." Katy clenches her hands together in her lap. Brian reaches over and holds one of them.

I've been there—not the assignment of bridesmaids, obviously, but the lack of close friends. My school friends drifted away, and I had no one close—until we formed a book club. "You should join my book club. They've become my closest friends. They're all wonderful, and I don't know what I would do without them."

Katy gives me a shy smile. "I'd love that."

Brian smiles at me too.

When I turn back around, Brody winks at me. It's like they're both telling me good job, but it makes me realize I've been remiss. I need to make more of an effort to get to know Katy. She's part of my family now too.

Katy gasps. She's staring at her phone with wide eyes and her mouth open. *Please tell me her mother hasn't found out she's eloping.* She's likely to call in a bomb threat to stop the plane.

"What's the matter, babe?"

"I checked our flight to see if it's on time, and it says we've been upgraded to first-class seats. Do you think it's a mistake?"

Brian frowns. "Must be."

Brody clears his throat. "Not a mistake. Consider it a wedding present."

Katy squeals.

"Dude..." Brian shakes his head. "Thanks, man."

"Don't mention it."

*How did Brody afford first-class tickets?* He said his parents disowned him a long time ago. His music must be doing well. That makes sense. I've only heard him that one time, but he's amazingly talented. And he was in Nashville for work.

He's going places. There's no chance he's staying in Granite Cove.

The little flame of hope that he might stay past the summer is snuffed out.

# Chapter Twenty-Two

The lights of the city glow in all directions. Every color of the rainbow is represented in the lights shining up and down the strip and beyond. I place my hand on the window of my hotel room. The room Brody booked for me—and wouldn't let me pay him for—is high up enough that I can see for miles in every direction. There's a show going on in the fountain in front of the hotel. Dozens of people stop to watch. The four of us caught a show this afternoon on the way to the chapel.

Brian and Katy are married. My little brother is now a husband. I smile and trace a small heart on the glass. They didn't have an Elvis impersonator for their wedding, even though Brian gave a half-hearted plea for one. Katy got her wish for the royal theme. Brian's borrowed king costume was a little ill fitting, but Katy's gown fit her beautifully. The two of them beamed at each other the entire time. I rub my cheeks. I've smiled so much today that they hurt.

A knock sounds on the door, and I whirl around. Brian and Katy are off enjoying their mini honeymoon, so it can't be them. *And I'm not going to speculate what they're doing.* But Brian made it clear we wouldn't see them until it was time for our flight home tomorrow.

*Did Brody change his mind about waiting to start our fling?* I peek through the hole in the door, but I don't see anyone. *Did I imagine the knock? Wishful thinking?* Brody and I separated when Brian and Katy said they were going up to their room. I had hoped Brody would suggest we have dinner together, but he seems to be taking keeping the secret seriously.

The knock sounds again, and I turn to the door on the other side of the room. Someone is knocking on the connecting door. *Did Brody get connecting rooms?*

*Or is some stranger knocking on the door?* With my luck, a serial killer or human trafficker would be on the other side. I lay my ear against the door. If I ask if it's him, whoever it is might muffle his voice and say yes.

My phone signals an incoming text, and I walk across the room to grab it from my nightstand.

*Brody: Where are you?*

*Me: In my room. Where are you?*

*Brody: Why didn't you open the door?*

I unlock and fling open the door. Brody leans against the wall, still dressed in his navy shirt and black dress pants, which cup his derriere just right. Earlier, the preacher caught me staring at Brody's ass and told me they had another opening for a wedding later tonight. I was afraid I was going to spontaneously combust from mortification on the spot. Luckily, Brian and Katy were so wrapped up in each other they were oblivious. Brody simply raised his eyebrow at me, and his adorable dimple nearly caused me to swoon.

*And here he is, right next door.* "I was worried you were a serial killer. Why didn't you tell me we had connecting rooms?"

Shaking his head, he grins. "I thought I had."

"I would've remembered that little detail."

"Oh yeah?" He puts his hands on my waist and leans down to kiss me. "Since Brian and Katy will be occupied until our flight, I thought it would be safe for you and me to spend some time together."

I loop my arms around his neck. "What did you have in mind?" *Please let it involve one of our beds.*

"Are you hungry? We haven't had dinner."

That's true but not exactly what I was hoping for. I suppose I should eat something before my stomach growls like a monster unleashed and scares him away for good. "What are you in the mood for?"

His gaze scans over me. "Dangerous question. You look beautiful in this green dress. It was really hard to keep my eyes off you all day." He kisses the tip of my nose. "I miss your glasses, though. On the other hand, I can see the green of your eyes without them." Then he kisses my lips.

*Note to self: contacts are overrated. Wear glasses more often.*

Heat tingles through me. "We could get room service."

His lips caress mine, and our tongues join in the fun. *Or skip dinner altogether.*

"I like room service." His lips trail across my cheek and kiss below my ear. "Besides, I can't exactly go out in public like this. There are probably public indecency laws even in Las Vegas."

I tilt my head to give him greater access to the wonderful things he's doing to my neck. "What are you talking about? You look wonderful." *Gorgeous. Sexy as heck.* Maybe keeping him in the hotel room and all to myself is a good thing. I don't want any other women getting any ideas.

He raises his head and smirks at me. "Wonderful, huh? Thanks, but I was referring to a not-so-little problem I have around you." He glances down.

When I follow his gaze, heat washes over me like I've just stepped into an oven. Sometimes I can be so obtuse. I bite my lip. *Definitely not little.* "We should absolutely stay in. I wouldn't want you arrested." *Or accosted by hordes of women.*

Laughing, Brody tugs me closer. I can feel exactly how not little he is against my stomach. Wrapping my arms tighter around him, I kiss him like it might be my one and only chance to experience genuine passion —because I'm still terrified it might be.

Instead of feeling the heat of embarrassment on my face, I'm now feeling warm in other places. And tingly—very, very tingly.

Brody's hands move from my waist to my back, and I'm molded against him.

I delve my fingers into his blond hair as my breaths come quicker. *Would it scare him away if I wrapped my legs around him and rubbed against him like a dog in heat?* Probably. It's definitely too early in the relationship for that.

The ache builds, and I'm afraid I might pant—and beg.

He groans and backs me toward the bed while still kissing me.

*Hallelujah.*

The bed bumps the back of my knees at the same time as his hands clasp my hips. He lifts me onto the bed, and I lie back, staring at his swollen lips and missing the feeling of them on mine.

Brody's gaze scorches me as he stares at my body. In this moment, I feel beautiful and desired.

"Are you sure?"

I blink at him. *I'm sure that if it doesn't happen, I'm going to need a dozen bottles of wine and a pint of ice cream to help me recover.* "I'm sure. Are you?"

He looks at me like I've lost my mind and glances down at himself. "It's obvious how sure I am." He tosses a condom onto the bed next to me and lies over me.

I bite my lip over the delicious feeling of his warmth and weight.

He kisses me like I'm a precious gift he can't wait to unwrap. His hands move over me like I'm a sculpture and he's a blind man trying to see.

I can't hold back a gasp of pleasure.

His fingers trail up my thigh as he lifts my dress.

I attack the buttons on his shirt, and my fingers get caught between us.

He chuckles and rises long enough to remove his shirt and the tank he's wearing underneath it.

I get lost staring at his chest and abs. *He's a work of art.*

Insecurity rears its ugly head. I am nowhere near as toned. In fact, I'm not even sure I have muscles under my jiggles. They're certainly absent right now, because I feel boneless lying here.

Brody pulls my dress down over my arms and chest. It pools around my waist. "Beautiful," he whispers. His fingers trace over my collarbone and down between my breasts.

Pleasure makes me shiver.

Leaning down, he kisses the same path his fingers just took. I raise my hands and hold his head. His busy fingers remove the rest of my clothes while his mouth exposes nerves and feelings I didn't know existed.

My body is on the precipice of something I've only fantasized about but could never quite reach. I've lost all control over my movements and thoughts as ecstasy tightens my skin and explodes in my brain.

Brody kisses his way back up my body as I lie still, having what I can only think is an out-of-body experience.

Control returns to my limbs, and I wrap my arms around him as he kisses my shoulder. His body is so warm. I explore his chest and abs before reaching for the button on his pants. When I fumble with the clasp, his fingers take over the task. He kisses me once more before standing and removing his clothes. His heavy-lidded gaze ignites the cauldron of desire inside me once again. I get only a peek of his entire body before he's covering me once again and reaching for the condom.

I'm torn between exploring his body more and finding out what else he can make me experience. *And how he's possibly going to fit.* I'm not great with science, but there is cause for concern.

I gasp as he proves my worries are pointless. We definitely fit.

I clutch him to me and hold on for the ride as another orgasm hits me like a rogue wave.

His breath pants against my ear, and his low groan sends tingles of desire through my core.

*This day has officially become the best day ever.*

# Chapter Twenty-Three

My body craves sleep. I'm thankful Brody is driving us home instead of me. The night road hypnotizes my eyes into closing. The brief series of naps I got on the plane weren't enough. Brian and Katy whisper together in the back seat. I roll my head on the headrest and stare at Brody's profile. This is why I couldn't sleep on the plane. I was too busy watching him sleep. *How is it possible for a man to be addictive even when he's sleeping?* Brody glances my way and gives me the small smile that makes his dimple pop out.

It's like my reproductive organs stand up and salute every time he smiles at me like that. *Yup, I have it bad.* And if I don't get myself under control, Brian and Katy are going to catch on. I turn away, even though all I want to do is unhook my seat belt and crawl into his lap. That would be a dead giveaway—and as dangerous as hell and probably cause an accident. Instead, I stare out the passenger window.

Brody and I never left our rooms until it was time to meet Brian and Katy for the flight home. We ordered room service for dinner and breakfast. Another day or two would have been nice or at least one more night. Sharing a shower with him is definitely on my list of favorite memories and things to do again. I shift in my seat as my memories stir my arousal.

Time to think of something else—anything else.

"Katy, remind me to send you a copy of what we're reading in book club this month. It's not our typical selection. It's actually a journal Franny found buried on her property."

"Really? How did she find it? Who wrote it?"

I glance back at Katy's smiling face. Her head rests on Brian's shoulder. "I don't want to spoil it for you, so I won't give you too many details. Franny found it while they were doing renovations on her property. We're trying to figure out who the author is so we can find out what happened to her and why she buried her journal there."

"It wasn't from someone who lived there prior to your friend?"

"Not according to any of our research. The house was empty for a long time, and we're guessing the time frame is within those years, so she wasn't a guest of the owners."

"That's fascinating. You haven't been able to track her down online?"

"We don't have her full name. All we know is she called herself Linny. There are no town records, either, and we're pretty sure she wasn't a resident of Granite Cove, so we're having a hard time tracking her down."

"Is your friend the one who married that Hollywood guy? The director or producer or something?" Brody asks.

"Director. Yes, Mitch Atwater."

"Oh, I read about that wedding in the town paper. You're friends with her?" Katy bounces in her seat. "I love the last movie he made about the cop. I cried buckets, but it was so good."

"She's the one who owns the bakery in town, right?"

I nod at Brian. "Yes, the Sweet Spot."

"I love that place. We were going to have them do our cake." Katy holds Brian's arm and leans against his shoulder once again.

If she's at all disappointed that she won't have the traditional wedding or cake, it doesn't show. Brian and Katy have both been glowing the entire trip.

"They fixed up that estate on the lake, right? The big house in the cove around the bend from town?" Brody asks.

"That's the one. It's not too far from your parents' place, is it? I forgot you lived close to them." I'd never been to his parents' place, so it's not so odd, I guess.

"Yeah, I remember my aunt was obsessed with the place the summer she stayed with us."

"I don't remember you mentioning an aunt before."

Brody shrugs. "I only ever saw her that one summer. Didn't know she existed before then and never heard about her again."

"Her name wasn't Linny, was it?"

He smiles. "Close. Aislinn."

Linny could be a nickname for Aislinn. It was on my list of names. *What are the chances Brody's aunt is Linny?* My heart rate kicks up, and this time, it has nothing to do with Brody being a foot away from me. "Is your aunt your father's or mother's sister?"

"Mother's. Why?"

"Just curious." More like dying to know if his aunt could be the Linny from the journal. *What was his mother's name? Did I ever know it?* I only recall anyone referring to them as Mr. and Mrs. Jackson.

"What are your parents' names again?" *That was subtle, right?*

Brody glances at me, but before he can reply, Katy's head appears between the seats. "Could Brody's aunt could be the Linny from your journal?"

"Probably not, but it's best to rule it out, don't you think?"

Katy frowns and sits back. "How exciting would that be if it was?"

*You haven't read the journal yet.* If it is his aunt, then she had an affair with his father, and he has not only a cousin out there but also a half brother.

"William and Lilianne. Those are my parents' names."

*Bingo!* But to be fair, William is a common name. And his mother's name isn't Sassy. Which means his aunt is probably not Linny—unless Sassy was a nickname not based on her sister's first name. "Does your mother have a middle name?"

"Marie."

"I guess it's not her."

"The search continues. I can't wait to read the journal."

I send Katy an email with the journal attached. "You should have it now."

Katy's phone notifies her. "Got it."

"You can read it while I catch up on my sleep," Brian mumbles.

*What if Sassy was a derivative of Sissy?* Like she couldn't pronounce her *I*'s or something as a kid and called her sister Sassy instead of Sissy. Or maybe it's because of her sister's personality rather than her name.

"Is your aunt older or younger than your mother?"

Brody chuckles. "Still trying to make a connection with the journal, or are you just curious about my family?"

"Can't it be both?" I do want to know more about Brody and, by extension, his family. And yes, I'd really like to rule out that Linny is Brody's aunt because the ramifications are piling up in my head.

"Younger by several years."

*Succotash!*

"Do you have any cousins?"

"Not that I know of. Like I said, I only saw her that one summer, and I didn't exactly pay much attention. I was a teenager. I had better things to do. For all I know, she could be married with a bunch of kids."

"You're not curious? I mean, they would be your cousins."

Brody glances at me then turns back to the road. "Family doesn't mean the same thing to me as it means to you."

I raise my hand to take his but catch myself in time. Showing Brody compassion might be misconstrued and lead to questions. He glances at me like he knows exactly what I'm thinking and what I almost did.

We ride in silence for the last leg of our journey. The trip takes its toll on Brian and Katy. They're both yawning when Brody drops them off and we hug goodbye.

Brody takes my hand as soon as we back out of the driveway. "What else was in this journal? Why do you care so much about finding the author?"

I nibble on my lip. "You sure you want to know? If it somehow is your aunt, there are details you might not want to learn." *Like your father had an affair with her when she was only a teenager and your grandparents took her baby away.*

"That only makes me want to know more. You get that, right? Besides, I'm not exactly close to my family, and nothing you could say would surprise me."

*Don't be so sure about that.* "The journal was written when Linny was a teenager. She had an affair with a much older man, and she got pregnant and had a baby, which her family didn't let her keep."

"Unfortunately, that story doesn't sound that rare. Do you have any idea when the journal was written?"

"From the descriptions, we determined Linny would be around our parents' age now. From the music and TV shows she mentioned and the clothes, it all makes sense."

"Is that it? Because so far, what you've told me isn't so shocking—even if it turns out to be my aunt."

"What's your mother's maiden name?" *We could search for Aislinn and Brody's parents and see what turns up.*

"Soren."

I feel Brody's gaze on me. *What more should I tell him? If it's not his aunt, it doesn't matter what I tell him. But if it is, then he'll know his father had an affair with his aunt. Why would she have come back that summer when he was a teenager to stay with her awful sister and brother-in-law? Was she looking for information on her baby? Did she find him?*

I gasp. *Succotash! Succotash! Succotash!* I must be more tired than I thought not to have made the connection before now. *Brody could be her baby!*

Brody pulls into my driveway and parks, but he doesn't shut off the Jeep or make any moves to get out. I peek sideways at him.

"I'm a patient guy, Mon. We can sit here all night while you figure out how to tell me what you're trying so hard not to. I, for one, would much rather take you inside to bed before the sun comes up and you have to go to work."

*By bed he means sharing my bed and not going back to him sleeping in the guest room, right? And by taking me to bed he means sex before sleep? I hope.*

*Here goes nothing.* Hopefully, he'll still want to sleep with me after what I tell him. "The older man Linny had an affair with was her sister's husband."

He remains silent, staring back at me with no expression on his face. "Both my parents have had affairs. I doubt either one of them has been faithful a day in their lives."

"Oh." *Guess it wouldn't be as earth-shattering as I thought.* "You're not worried you could be the baby boy who was taken away from her?"

That gets a reaction out of him. His eyebrows shoot toward his hair-line. "It would explain why my mother hates me so much."

"Oh, Brody." I grab his hand.

"It's okay, Mon. I accepted it a long time ago. My parents have never had any familial feelings toward me. It would actually be a relief to learn I didn't belong to them, but then again, my aunt apparently didn't want me either."

"She did. In the journal, she was devastated when they took her baby."

"Then why did she come that summer then leave, never to be heard from again? She would've always known where I was. If she wanted me, she had plenty of opportunities."

"You're right. It doesn't make sense. Linny probably wasn't your aunt." That would be devastating to Brody. She would be one more person who didn't want him. And it doesn't mesh with the journal. That Linny would've come back for her baby.

"Good. Now that we solved that mystery, can we go inside? There are a lot better things I'd like to do with you than discuss my messed-up family."

"I'd like to hear about these things." *Better yet, I'd rather you show me.*

# Chapter Twenty-Four

Brody sits at the kitchen table. Instead of dinner, the table is covered with old photo albums, papers, and an open laptop. He barely glances at me when I walk in the door. There's no smile or greeting. Hank waddles over, wagging his tail. *At least someone is happy to see me.*

"Everything okay?"

He rubs his hands over his face and stretches his arms behind his head, then he slides the open photo album across the table. "I couldn't get the whole journal thing out of my head. I had Katy forward me the email you sent her and spent the morning reading it, then I went over to the lake house and did some digging. These are old photo albums my grandparents had." He taps the page. "Look what it says under this picture."

It's a photo of a girl and a woman. Underneath, someone wrote "Lily and Linny."

He scowls. "It's my mother and aunt. It's from my mother and father's engagement party. I don't have anything from my mother's side because her parents died when I was a kid. I doubt my mother saved any mementos, but if she did, I don't know where they are. It was a long shot, but I went into the attic to see if there might be anything with my aunt in them. My father's parents had all this stuff. She's in a few more pictures. My parents' wedding. Then nothing. There's not a single picture of her after the wedding or from that summer I remember her visiting. There's also not a single picture of my mother pregnant with me. Odd, right?"

I don't know what to say. Linny is Brody's aunt and possibly his birth mother.

"There's more. I can't find any trace of Aislinn Soren online for the past fifteen years. If I'm remembering correctly, that lines up with that summer."

"What are you saying?"

"I'm saying after that summer, she vanished."

"Or someone made her vanish."

He stares at me. "Or someone made her vanish."

*Are we really entertaining the notion that Brody's parents might've murdered his aunt or birth mother? Are they capable of that? Her own sister? The mother of his child?* "Brody, I think we might be getting ahead of ourselves here. We're jumping to a lot of conclusions. Do you really believe your parents are capable of murdering her? Because that's what we're basically saying, isn't it?"

Brody stands and paces into the living room and back. "I hate to say or even contemplate that they could, but I know how they are—especially when money is involved."

"What does money have to do with anything?"

He stops and puts his hands on his hips. "Any wealth my parents had came from their parents. Both sets of my grandparents were well-off. My father's family more so."

"So you think your mother agreed to raise you as her own for money? What would that have to do with Linny disappearing? You said her parents were deceased by then. Or do you think your father's parents were in on it too?"

He shakes his head. "My maternal grandparents left me a trust, but my parents spent it all before I was old enough to access it."

I suck in a breath. "Is that legal?"

"They had access until I turned twenty-one."

"You think that is their motive to get rid of your aunt." I can't quite bring myself to say *murder* out loud again. *Are we really standing here discussing it like some unsolved cold case I've watched on TV?*

"I also inherited the majority of my paternal grandparents' estate, including the lake house and their other properties my parents were living in. If they knew or even suspected, they had a double motive to keep her silent. I don't know if my grandparents knew about Linny and me or not. If they did, I haven't found any record of it. I'd like to believe they didn't. They were decent to me growing up. But if they were anything like my other grandparents, maybe they made their financial support a condition of keeping the secret."

Brody's rich. I mean, I knew he grew up wealthy, but when he said his parents disowned him and he had to make his own way, I assumed the money stayed gone. It was never his parents' money to begin with, though. They were basically using Brody as their meal ticket. "What if your paternal grandparents didn't know? Doesn't it provide even more of a motive for them to keep it quiet? You said they were living off your grandparents' largess. That could be taken away. And if your parents weren't aware, you would inherit the estate, and they assumed they would..."

"It would give them even more motive."

"What do you want to do now?"

"Like you said, it's all circumstantial. I want to confront them face-to-face. I want to see their reaction."

"Are you crazy? We just stood here discussing the possibility that your parents might've gotten rid of your aunt, and you want to confront them with it? What are you going to say? Hi, Mom and Dad. Did you kill off your sister-slash-baby-momma?"

His lips twitch.

*How the heck can he find this funny?* If it were my parents, I'd be going out of my mind.

Brody pulls me into his arms and hugs me. "First, I've never called them Mom and Dad. It was always Mother and Father. Second, they're practically strangers to me. I sign off on their annual allowance once a year, and that's it. I haven't spoken to them in person since the will was read. And considering their reaction then, I doubt they had a clue my grandparents had left everything to me."

"You give them an allowance?"

"It was easier to keep my grandparents' method in place. They gave them an allowance every year too. I just kept it going."

"Why?"

"Why do you do so much for your parents? They're the parents, yet you act like you are most of the time. And I know when we were kids you held a lot of the responsibility for Brian."

He's right, but his parents were awful to him.

"I didn't do it out of the kindness of my heart or anything. It kept them off my back. And they would've tried everything to keep me drowning in court battles. I gave them the choice of taking the allowance or nothing."

"They threatened you with court when the will was read?"

"No, actually, that came after. First, they threatened to kill me."

My jaw drops.

Brody rolls his eyes. "They demanded I give them what they thought was rightfully theirs, which I refused. Mother mumbled something about how she should've drowned me as a baby. Father tried to punch me, which I easily dodged, then he asked the lawyer what would happen if I died. The lawyer told him they wouldn't get a penny. I made sure of that by having a will drawn up when I found out they drained my trust fund."

"You can't confront those people. There is no telling what they might do."

"They kill me, their lifestyle goes away."

"You expose them, it goes away anyway because they go to prison."

# Chapter Twenty-Five

My heart aches as I leave Brody home alone, but I promised Brian I would be with him and Katy to tell our parents about the elopement. Brody assured me he would hold off on confronting his parents until we found concrete proof the Linny in the journal was his aunt Aislinn and possibly his birth mother. But it's been two days, and I can tell his patience is dissolving like the ice in my cup when I pour hot coffee over it.

Thank the lord I finally got him to agree to let me inform the book-club ladies about our suspicions so they could help research. I can understand his wanting to keep it secret until we know for sure, but the more minds we have working on this, the more likely we are to come up with results. The ladies were shocked and excited at the same time. Finding the Linny in the journal has consumed all of us. And as Lucinda pointed out, we ladies are well-versed in not only keeping secrets but uncovering family skeletons as well. *Would it help Brody to talk to Bobby and Lucinda?* Bobby might have some insights for him because of what he went through with his own family. Then again, Brody already thinks the worst of his parents and has no contact with them.

After reading the journal, I wanted to find out what happened to Linny and her baby. I wanted to know she had a happy life. Now, all I worry about is how all this is going to affect Brody. *I certainly don't wish her dead, but if she's not, then where has she been all these years? Why would she let her son be raised by the very people who betrayed her?*

My parents' house comes into view. I need to put all these thoughts on hold. Brian asked me here for support. Our parents will be happy for him in the long run, but they might be a little hurt they didn't get to witness the wedding themselves. On the other hand, they might only be ecstatic. All the wedding drama is over, and Brian and Katy are happy. That's the important part I hope everyone can remember. *I don't envy Katy's talk with her parents.* That is bound to be unpleasant. *More like a gut-wrenching, soul-crushing confrontation.*

Brian's truck is already in the driveway. As I pull in, he gets out. *Did he wait for me or just get here? Is he that worried about our parents' reaction?* Katy gets out of the passenger side. It's good they're doing this together. They're a team now. It's important for them to stand united. Katy is definitely going to need Brian standing beside her when they tell her parents.

"Hey, newlyweds."

They both smile and give me hugs.

"Thanks for being here. You're always better at smoothing things over with them. I don't want to upset them, but they need to know this was our decision."

"That's exactly what they need to hear." I squeeze their hands. "They'll be happy for you."

Brian nods.

"My parents won't be." Katy grimaces and chews on her fingernail.

"When do you plan to tell them?"

"Tomorrow." Katy looks at the house. "We thought your parents might be good practice and less likely to make a scene."

"I could go with you if you think it will help." *Oh my lord, why did I say that?* I'd rather walk naked down the street than have to deal with those unpleasant people again, but Katy said she doesn't have any friends.

Brian snorts. "Considering you looked like you were ready to leap across the table and strangle Deborah, I doubt you could be your usual calming influence."

*Point taken.* And here I thought I had managed to keep my rage contained.

Katy hugs my arm. "Thank you for offering. Brian has always said what a wonderful sister you are, and I'm tickled pink I get to call you my sister now too."

I bump her shoulder with mine. "I'm happy we're sisters now too. And if you need anything, even if it has to do with your parents, I'm here for you."

The front door opens, and my mother stands in the doorway. "What are you all doing standing outside?" She peers upward. "The forecast says rain."

I look up at the blue sky, which has only a handful of light-gray clouds mixed in with the white. If the weatherman tells my mother there's a chance of rain or snow, then it's a guarantee she's not leaving the house.

Brian holds the door for us as we go inside.

Dad comes out of the kitchen, smiling. "To what do we owe this pleasure?"

I glance at Brian and Katy. *Did they rehearse how they're going to break the news? They aren't planning on my telling them, are they? Succotash! I should've asked what the plan was.*

"Katy and I eloped in Vegas." Brian holds up their hands with their wedding rings on display.

*Okay, not exactly the way I would've chosen.* I would've started with what led to the decision.

Mom and Dad stare at the rings silently.

My mother breaks the silent stare first with a gasp. She covers her mouth with her hands, and tears fill her eyes.

*Oh no, is this going to break her? Should I have consulted with her therapist beforehand? Why didn't I think of that before now?*

When she opens her arms and hugs Brian and Katy at the same time, my whole body sags with relief. Dad claps Brian on the back while he waits his turn to join the hugging.

Brian catches my gaze over our parents' heads and smiles. I smile back. This is good. All parties are happy. I refuse to think about Katy's parents. They're not my concern.

"Vegas!" Mom gasps again. "You went to Las Vegas?"

"It was so much fun!" Katy claps.

"Come sit and tell us all about it," Dad says and waves everyone over to the couches and chairs.

I perch on the armchair as Katy recites all the highlights of the trip, focusing on the wedding. She shows them the pictures on her phone, and I make a note to send her the ones I took. When Mom and Dad hear I went along on the trip, they both stare at me with wide eyes.

After the retelling, Mom leads Brian and Katy into the kitchen so they can help her put the photos on her phone. I stand to follow. Mom will want to make sure everyone is fed, so I'll fix some snacks while they concentrate on the phone and revel in the happiness.

"Honey, hold up."

I glance at Dad.

He points at the chair I just vacated, and I sit back down. He probably wants assurances that this is what Brian and Katy really wanted and not an impulsive result of the wedding drama.

"We need to talk about why you thought offering to pay for the wedding was a good idea."

*Succotash! Now? He wants to discuss this now?*

Brian and Katy laugh in the kitchen, and I hear the fridge open and close while Mom offers them food and drink.

"Monica?"

I toss my hands into the air. "I was trying to keep the peace, Dad. I thought it was the best way to stop the Lewises' attacks and keep Brian out of it." *How was I supposed to know Deborah wasn't capable of keeping her mouth shut or from spewing more hatred?*

*Stupid question.* The woman's previous actions should have made that very clear to me.

Dad's face crumples. "I realize we've leaned on you too much. You shouldn't have to feel the need to protect us or your brother."

Tears fill my eyes, and I stare at the floor.

Mom walks back in. "Brian and Katy are having a snack in the kitchen. Poor things didn't eat dinner. Monica, are you... What's going on?"

I feel her gaze on me. By a "snack," she probably means she emptied the refrigerator and there's now a spread of food on the counter. "I'm good, Mom."

"I'm talking to Monica about her plan to pay our half of the wedding and whatever else she promised the Lewises."

"Oh." Mom places her hand on my shoulder. "We know your heart was in the right place."

"Monica, your mother and I did you a disservice. You were always so responsible that we took it for granted and let you take on too much."

Mom sits next to Dad on the couch. "I know it was hard for you when I was... ill."

Squeezing Mom's hand clenched in her lap, Dad continues, "You were always more like a second mother to Brian than a sister. And it seemed like it was in your nature to care for people. But we took advantage."

"No, you didn't. I wanted to help. I needed to."

Mom and Dad's faces are etched with concern as they stare at me.

I rub my damp hands down my pants.

"Is this about Rosie?" Mom whispers. "You were always the responsible one, but you became even more so after Rosie. I knew I was failing you then, but I couldn't get past my grief."

"Mom, you didn't fail me. I... I wasn't sick that day. I pretended to be so I could stay home with the bunny Rosie and I got for our birthday. If I hadn't, Rosie would never have been in that car."

"Oh, honey, no." Mom hurries over and wraps her arms around me. "I knew you weren't sick. Rosie monopolized the bunny, so I thought it would be okay for you to have some alone time with it. And I was tired. I tried to convince Rosie to skip gymnastics that day, but she was adamant. She always knew exactly what she wanted. You're not to blame. You were never to blame."

"I can't believe you've been blaming yourself all these years." Dad shakes his head. "Why didn't you tell us?"

"I was afraid. Afraid you would blame me too."

My father's gaze is blurry through my tears, but I can see the ones on his cheeks. "Rosie was a force of nature even in the short time she had on earth. She lived it to the fullest. She was a handful. I loved her with all my heart, and I miss her every single day. You were always the calm, well-behaved one. So maybe we didn't look close enough to see how much you were hurting. Like your mother said, we were both wrapped up in our own grief. We let you put way too much on your shoulders. I'm sorry—so deeply sorry."

Mom wipes the tears from my face with a tissue then wipes her own. "No one was to blame. We could play the blame game over and over, and it won't change anything. I blamed myself for many years too. There's always going to be a missing part of my heart, but I'm finally realizing I need to go on living. If I don't, who's going to remember all the joy she brought? I don't want to miss any more life, and I don't want you to either. You have such a beautiful soul, honey. Don't let the past take away from your future."

A heavy hand squeezes my shoulder, making me look up. Brian bends down and kisses me on the head. "We've all been walking on too many eggshells. I don't remember Rosie as much as I'd like to. I always felt guilty for not grieving as hard as any of you. I guess I avoided talking about her because of it. But I'd like to hear stories about her." He smiles. "I do remember her hogging that bunny, though. She wouldn't even let me hold it."

My phone buzzes in my lap as we all chuckle.

"Why is Brody asking when you're coming home or saying that he misses you?" Brian growls above my head.

"I knew there were sparks flying back and forth between the two of you!" Katy claps in the kitchen doorway.

All eyes are on me.

"He had a flood. He needed a place to stay."

Mom pats my arm. "That was kind of you to let him stay with you."

Dad stares at me, and I squirm in my seat. "Something going on between the two of you?"

*Should I lie?* No, he'll know if I lie. I turn as red as ketchup anytime I do. *How can I deflect this?*

"Son of a bitch!" Brian stalks across the living room and back.

*Why is he so angry?*

He stops in front of me. "I love him like a brother, but he's not good enough for you. You deserve to have someone who will always put you first. He'll never do that."

Mom and Dad share looks. Dad stands. "Brian."

"He's going to break her heart."

# Chapter Twenty-Six

My brain replays Brian dragging Katy out of the house while I stand there speechless like a movie clip stuck on a loop. I was too shocked and embarrassed to explain that what Brody and I have is a summer fling, and I'm well aware he's not going to fall in love with me. My parents kept asking me if I was all right and if I wanted to stay. I don't even know what I mumbled to them. And I sure as heck don't know what I'm going to say to Brody. We agreed to keep our fling a secret, and now Brian not only knows but is also mad. Brody had joked that Brian warned him away from me years ago, but I never dreamed Brian would be so angry or react the way he did.

I glance in the rearview and side mirrors before I put the car in reverse and back out of my parents' driveway. I hope something intelligent will pop into my head before I get home. Brody already has enough on his plate with the Linny mystery.

My phone beeps with an incoming text message.

*Katy: Brian is pissed. He dropped me off and is on his way to your house to confront Brody.*

*Succotash! Succotash! Succotash! What am I going to do?*

My backup alarm screams out a series of beeps. My eyes almost pop out of my head when I spot my parents' mailbox inches from my bumper. I slam on the brakes. Thank the lord I wasn't going fast. *Gee, Mom and Dad. So sorry I ran over your mailbox after dumping all the drama on you tonight.* I pull forward and turn the wheel so I can back up straight this time.

I check off Katy's text so she knows I received it. *What is Brian thinking?* He's going to ruin everything. I don't need my little brother protecting my heart. I know exactly what I'm doing.

*Don't I?*

*Should I call Brian and try to reason with him or call Brody and warn him? Brody first then Brian.*

Brody's phone rings and rings. *Pick up. Please pick up.*

His voicemail answers. "Brian is on his way over. He found out about us and is upset. I'm so sorry! I'm on my way."

Maybe he went out for something and he won't be there when Brian gets there.

Next, I dial Brian, but he doesn't pick up either. "Brian, stop and call me back. Do not confront Brody. I know exactly what I'm doing. You don't need to protect me. Please. Call me." *Will he listen to his voicemail before he goes in?*

*How long will it take Brian to get there?* If he just dropped off Katy, then I should make it home before he gets there—barely. But if Katy waited to text me and he had a few minutes' head start, then he could make it there first.

If I pull over to text them both, then I'll waste more time. *If I text while driving and get in an accident...* I chomp down on my bottom lip so hard that it makes me wince. I hit buttons while my gaze darts back and forth between the road and my phone, then I finally get the microphone to come up in a text to Brody. "Brody, Brian is on his way. Check your voicemail. I promise I'll handle him. Don't open the door."

I roll my eyes as I swipe up and close the screen. *Yeah, right. Like he's going to stand there and not open the door to Brian.*

Brian's next. "Do not. I repeat, do not go to my house, Brian Frasier! Mind your own business."

*Am I hyperventilating?* My chest is tight and rising and falling with my rapid breaths. I place my hand on it and take as deep of a breath as I can. *Why is my boring life suddenly so riddled with drama?*

*Wait. Did I manifest this by complaining about how boring my life was?* Perfect. Sounds about right.

*Succotash! Succotash! Succotash!* Brian's truck is in my driveway.

As soon as I open my car door, I hear Brian yelling. There's a crash, and I almost trip over my feet on the walk. *Oh my god! They're physically fighting?* I stumble up the stairs and throw open the door.

Brody has Brian in a headlock, and Brian is punching Brody in the side.

"Stop!" I scream at the top of my lungs.

Brody raises his arms and shoves Brian away from him. Brian stumbles several steps back then lunges toward him again.

I jump between them. "Don't you dare!"

Brody grabs me by the waist and puts me behind him.

Brian narrows his eyes and shoves his finger in Brody's chest. "Keep your damn hands off my sister!"

"That should be up to your sister, shouldn't it?"

I shove my way back between them. "Brian, you remember when you told me you were a grown-ass man and to stop meddling in your business? Well, right back at you. I'm a grown-ass woman. I know what I'm doing. And you and I clearly need to have another long lecture about fighting never solving anything. I thought you outgrew this proclivity." Too many conversations on this topic when he was a teenager flash through my mind.

Brian's face is red. "You're not thinking clearly. He's manipulating you. He's a player. He never sticks. Hell, he doesn't even live in one place. He travels all over, playing his music. You going to become a groupie now and follow him like a lovesick fool? 'Cause I promise you, you won't be alone. He's left a long line of broken hearts. Hell, women throw themselves at him. I've seen it with my own eyes. You going to join them? Did he tell you any of that? Or did he just make you empty promises?"

His words are like arrows to my heart. *Since when did my little brother consider me a helpless, naive woman who would let herself be manipulated by a handsome face? Does he think I'm stupid?* "Brody hasn't made me any promises. In fact, he's asked me time and again if I was sure. I guess that makes me the aggressor. I went after him. And I'm more than well aware it's temporary. He's only here for the summer. I had no idea you had such a low opinion of me and your best friend."

Brian glares at Brody over my shoulder then switches his gaze back to me. "You." He shakes his head. "You went after him? Even knowing he'd be gone in a few weeks? For what? Sex? You're lying. You're not that kind of woman. You're protecting him."

"I'm not what kind of woman? A woman who likes sex? Well, brother dear, I've got news for you. I'm exactly that kind of woman. What is so wrong with my having a relationship even though I know it's temporary? Are you actually going to stand there and tell me every woman you've had sex with, you thought you might marry some day? I know for a fact that's not true. And I'm sure Brody could testify to the fact because the two of you went through a swath of women the summers he was here."

Brian turns impossibly redder. "It's not the same. That dick, Aaron, already broke your heart once, and I couldn't protect you. I'll be damned if I'll stand by and watch my best friend break your heart again. You can say you know what you're doing all you want, but I know you. You don't fall into bed with a guy unless your feelings are involved." He points at Brody while staring at me. "You going to lie to my face and tell me your heart's not going to be broken when he leaves? That some part of you isn't hoping he'll stay?"

He might as well have gutted me. The result would be the same.

"Aaron didn't break my heart. He broke my pride. And knowing something is going to hurt isn't a reason not to live. I am so sick of making choices in my life to satisfy everyone else. When does it get to be my time? If I keep deciding to protect my heart, then I might as well give up now. A chance at happiness is better than no chance at all." I close my eyes to stem the tears. "I can't lie and tell you I feel nothing. I know it's going to hurt. I've accepted that. It's my choice, Brian, and you need to accept it. You're my brother, and I love you, but you're the one hurting me right now."

The tears in my brother's eyes nearly shatter me completely. "I'll be here to pick up the pieces when he breaks your heart." He kisses me on my cheek and leaves.

I watch the door close behind him and hear his truck start and drive away all without moving a muscle. Brody doesn't speak or move either.

Hank butts against my leg as he waddles by and jumps onto the couch. I don't blame him for hiding from all the anger and noise. The cowardly part of me wants to do the same.

"I want to argue and say what he said was all lies. But I'd be the one lying if I said it didn't hurt like hell that my best friend thinks so little of me."

Swinging around, I shake my head. "It's not about you. It's not. He's being overly protective. He'll feel bad for his words tomorrow. Brian doesn't always think things through before he acts or speaks. I know my brother."

Brody gives me a sad smile. "So do I." He stares at the door behind me. "I never wanted to hurt you, Mon."

"I know. You didn't." *You will, and with the way you're staring at the door, it's going to be sooner rather than later.*

"But you expect I will because that's what I do."

"No." I reach for his arm, but he steps back, and my heart clenches. "It's not what you do." He's not responsible for feelings he doesn't feel. *He can't make himself love me.*

"I need to go."

"Brody..."

He pauses at the door. "I'm sorry."

# Chapter Twenty-Seven

Hank licks my hand and sticks his nose in my face. *Probably checking to see if I'm still alive.* I stare at the dog toy under the couch. Hank likes hiding his toys around the house, under the furniture. He sniffs at me once again. I should reassure him I'm okay, but I don't want to lie to the dog. It's not like he's likely to believe me anyway. When his human lies on the floor, not moving, it's probably a clear sign something is wrong. When that human also has her face pressed into the area rug, which is drenched in her tears, there's probably cause for concern.

So much for a summer fling. It was more like a few days. *Shouldn't it hurt less since it was less time? What would I have been like if we had lasted the summer?*

So this is what a broken heart feels like. I could've gone without experiencing this kind of pain. I curl into a tighter ball. *I wish Rosie were here.* She could always make the hurt go away.

I thought if I knew and accepted it was just temporary, I could protect my heart. *Who knew you could deceive yourself?* I was already in love with Brody by the time I convinced myself I could handle an affair. *How did I miss the signs?*

Hank lies next to me, and I pet his head as the minutes tick by. My tears dry, but I still can't summon the energy to drag myself off the floor.

Rationally, I know I'll survive this. I have to. There are two days left of the school year. I can wallow in my misery once summer officially begins. I'll schedule it in my calendar. *Today, you can break down and sob like a baby.* I'm probably going to need more than one day. *All right, this week, you can wallow and cry.* I've been through worse, and I'll survive this too.

*You knew this was coming. It shouldn't be such a surprise. Push the feelings away and bury them. Just for two more days.* I look at my watch. Ten more minutes, then I'm getting up. I scrub my cheeks and roll onto my back. *You're a strong, capable, smart woman. You're a survivor. This will not break you.*

Hank raises his head when I sit up and stares at me like he's checking to see if I'm going to make it. I pat him on the head. *Jury is still out.*

He follows me to the bathroom and watches from the door as I splash water on my face. I look across the hall into the guest room. Brody's guitar leans in the corner. He didn't take any of his things. I look down at Hank. Or his dog. *I'm keeping the dog.* It's only fair. Possession matters. Hank has been living with me. Call it a consolation prize. I doubt Brody will argue. Guilt won't let him.

I step into the room to find his duffel is open on the bed. He's been sharing my bedroom since we came back from Vegas, but he never moved anything into it. *Will he abandon his things to avoid me? Text and ask me to leave them on the steps?* No, he'll come by during the day while I'm at school. I'll come home to find all his things gone like he was never here.

*Keeping a memento is normal.* I pick up a blue T-shirt. He was wearing this yesterday, and I sniff it to see if I can still smell him. *Might be edging into creepy now.* I don't care. It does smell like him. I choke on my tears, and my chest shudders. Sitting on the bed, I hold the shirt against my chest. Hank sits on the floor in front of me with his head cocked to the side. He's probably thinking, *What's this crazy lady doing now?*

A notebook sits on top of his clothes inside the open duffel. It's flipped open, so it's not like I'm invading his privacy if I read what's written. It's a song.

. . .

"Perfection"

*Baby you're perfection*
*Give me a chance*
*I can be the man for you*
*This can't be our last dance*
*I'll break all my bad habits too*


*Your beauty takes my breath away*
*Your heart is a rare gift*
*You keep all my demons at bay*


*Your laugh warms my soul*
*Heals all the pain*
*And makes me whole*


*Baby you're perfection*
*Give me a chance*
*I can be the man for you*
*This can't be our last dance*
*I'll break all my bad habits too*


*I need you like I need to breathe*
*You're in my every thought*
*All I want to do is make you smile*
*This kind of love can't be bought*


*You walk in a room and my heart races*
*I love staring at you*

*And discovering something new*


*Baby you're perfection*
  *Give me a chance*
  *I can be the man for you*
  *This can't be our last dance*
  *I'll break all my bad habits too*


*One look that's all it took*
  *I fell hard and never recovered*
  *I want to make all your dreams come true*
  *Tell me you feel it too*


My tears dampen the page, and I flip to the next one, which is full of music notes. I've never wished so hard I was able to read music. He may not love me, but he's loved someone—or maybe he's just really good at faking it. I read over the words again and feel a small twinge of envy for whoever inspired the words. *I want to be loved like that. I want Brody to love me like this.*

Hank waddles out of the room. *Yeah, buddy. I don't blame you. I'm tired of me too.* I rub my hand over the notebook in my lap while the fingers of my other hand rub the T-shirt.

The feeling of being watched spills over me, and I look up. Brody stands in the doorway. My breath stutters in my chest. *He came back!*

His gaze rakes over me and lands on his things in my hands.

*Is that why he's here? For his things?* I glance down at his notebook and T-shirt crumpled in my fist. "I can explain." *Yeah, go ahead. I'm waiting. This should be good.* Confessing I was smelling his shirt or using it as some sort of soothing mechanism like a kid with a blankie will not paint me in a sane or normal light. Neither will telling him I want to keep it as a memento. He's bound to notice if I stuff it under my shirt or sit on it so he doesn't take it when he gathers his things. Instead, I just shrug. *I've got nothing.*

"I shouldn't have left like that."

Looking at him is too hard and raw. He doesn't need to see me bursting into tears. I'm sure the evidence of my breakdown is all over my face anyway.

"You deserve better—so much better."

Ah, he came back to give me the "It's not you, it's me" speech. Sadly, I've heard that one before.

"I lied to you."

That brings my gaze to him. *What did he lie about?*

He stuffs his hands into his front pockets. "My house didn't flood." He looks at Hank sitting at his feet. "I got Hank as an excuse to spend time with you too. Brian was right. I manipulated you."

"I don't understand." *Is he saying he lied to be closer to me? Move in with me? Why?*

"You weren't exactly receptive to my attempts at flirting and getting you to go out with me and see me as something other than your little brother's pesky friend. So I manufactured reasons to be with you, hoping you'd give me a chance."

I cast my eyes down to his notebook still in my lap.

"Yes, the song is about you. All my songs lately are." He sighs. "A lot of my earlier stuff is too."

"I'd like to hear them sometime." The words on the page waver. *If he did all that to be close to me, then why did he leave? Did he decide I wasn't worth the trouble? Was it just the chase? He caught me and that was the end?*

Brody squats in front of me. "You called this just a summer fling. You already had an end date in mind. I want a chance to prove I can be more. I'm not sure if I'm boyfriend material. You deserve better. Maybe I'm being selfish. But I'd still like to try."

*I hurt him by saying it was temporary?* "I... I thought that was all you were offering. It never occurred to me you wanted more." *He's going to stay?*

"And now that you know?"

I search Brody's face. *How is it possible this beautiful man wants me? How can he doubt my feelings for an instant? Have all my insecurities made me completely blind to the wonder in front of me?*

"I've tried so hard to go slowly and gently when all I want to do is make you mine, but we can go as slowly as you need. I promise I'll be patient. I'll move back to my house, and we'll go on dates."

I throw myself against him, and we fall to the floor with his arms wrapped around me. "Don't you dare. I don't want you to leave. I want you here. I'd still like the dates though."

His chuckle warms my ear, and his arms wrap tighter around me. "I can do that."

I lift my head. "What does *not* slow and gentle look like?"

He grins before devouring my mouth and rolling me beneath him. His hands are everywhere, removing my clothes and igniting passion. He makes me breathless. His lips never fully leave mine as he removes his clothes. As soon as we're skin to skin, his tongue possesses mine like he's starving for me. We both gasp and moan when we're joined. I desperately want to keep staring at his beautiful face, but my eyes drift closed as the pleasure becomes too much. Lights dance behind my eyelids, and my body arches.

"You are so damn beautiful," he whispers into my ear.

# Chapter Twenty-Eight

Brody types on his laptop while I lie next to him in his bed, watching him while I'm supposed to be paying attention to the book-club ladies' text string. Barbara is updating us on the latest matchmaking disaster Aunt Aggie and Sally set her up with. Thank the lord I never agreed to let them try their harebrained idea on me. I glance out his bedroom window at the lake view. Over the past couple of weeks, we've been splitting our time between his house and mine. I'm not sure which one I prefer more. It's probably equal as long as we're together.

His tan skin is a sharp contrast to the white sheet bunched across his waist. My gaze follows the narrow path of hair over his abdomen to his chest.

"You keep looking at me like that, and I'm never going to finish this email."

Grinning, I meet his gaze, and he lifts the laptop off his lap. "Never mind. It can wait."

"No." I put my hand on the screen. "Finish the email. My fantasies will hold a few more minutes."

"How do you expect me to concentrate on this when you're lying there all sexy and admitting you have fantasies you need me to fulfill?" He leans forward far enough to kiss me.

Laughing, I put my hand on his chest. "What do you have so far?"

He sits back and frowns at the screen. "The email address is probably long defunct, if they were even telling the truth when they gave it to me."

"It might be, but isn't it worth it to try?" The thought of his parents and what they tried to pull when he reached out to them makes me want to clobber both of them while I give them a piece of my mind. They were openly hostile to Brody even before he brought up the subject of Aislinn. He made up a story about finding some of her belongings and wanting to return them to her. After demanding to know what it was and insisting anything of value should belong to them, they tried to barter an increase in their allowance for information. Brody countered with eliminating their allowance altogether if they didn't tell him what they knew. All they gave him was an old email for her they hadn't used in years. They made no mention of Brody being her biological child or where she disappeared to. It's hard to know if they were being secretive, there's nothing to reveal, or they're so narcissistic it simply didn't occur to them to mention.

Brody sighs. "Aunt Aislinn, I would like to speak to you. If this email reaches you, please contact me." He turns the screen toward me. "Other than my name and contact information, that's all I've come up with."

"I like it. It's short and to the point, and you don't reveal any information. Since we still have more questions than answers right now, it's perfect."

He hits Send. "Now, weren't you about to tell me something about a fantasy?" He puts his laptop on the floor next to the bed and reaches for me as my phone buzzes in my hand.

*Rebecca: Not to hijack the matchmaking update, but what's everyone found out about Linny or Aislinn?*

I wince at Brody as he hesitates with his hands on my waist. "They want an update on Linny. Can I tell them about the email?"

"Go ahead." He lifts me onto his lap.

I gasp and laugh as I reach for the sheet while holding my phone.

*Monica: Brody just emailed an address his parents gave him. They said it was for his aunt. I guess we just have to wait and see.*

*Lucinda: Came across some news clippings from the town where Brody's mother and sister (whichever is which) grew up.*

Screenshots come across next, and I expand them as Brody and I peer at my screen. One is a wedding announcement for Brody's parents. It mentions Aislinn in attendance. Another is Brody's birth announcement, which does not mention Aislinn. The last is an obituary for Brody's grandparents. It says they are survived by daughters Lilianne and Aislinn and grandson Brody.

"Doesn't tell us much." Brody leans back on his pillow, and I snuggle against his chest.

"Unless they're lying, it means your aunt was still alive when her parents died."

"We've already established we can't trust anything my parents say. They would've said that to avoid any questions of her whereabouts."

*Franny: Mitch offered to hire a private investigator, but considering we suspect Linny is Aislinn, I said we need Brody's permission.*

"What do you think?"

Brody shrugs. "If he's willing, I guess it can't hurt."

*Monica: Brody says go for it.*

Franny sends a clapping emoji.

*Rebecca: You responded very quickly, Monica. Does that mean this mysterious Brody, who none of us have yet met, is close by?*

*Lucinda: Yes, Monica, when are we going to meet your new beau?*

Brody snickers and moves his hands under the sheet, down my body. "Very close by."

Laughing, I swat at his hand. "I can't concentrate when you do that."

"That is the point. Tell them they can come over here this afternoon."

"You sure?" *Does he really want to be invaded by all my friends at once?* I'd offer to include Brian so there's someone Brody knows, but while Brian is no longer openly hostile, he hasn't fully accepted Brody and me dating either.

"Absolutely. That gives me a few hours to make all your fantasies come true."

I giggle and send the text, inviting them. However, I add a couple of hours for recovery time.

# Chapter Twenty-Nine

Brody kisses the back of my neck as I wash the last dish. "What do you say we get out of here today and clear our heads?" He takes the dish from me after I rinse it and begins drying it.

"What do you have in mind?" We have been sort of hibernating in either his house or mine lately. "Last night wasn't too much socializing for you?" A few of the book-club ladies stopped by for an impromptu get-together. Brody handled all their less-than-subtle interrogation with his usual charm. Technically, it was our first hosting event as a couple, and I think it went pretty well.

*Couple.* That word still feels a little surreal. Brody and are a couple. Giddiness makes my lips twitch.

"Wasn't really talking about socializing with anyone. I just meant the two of us getting some fresh air. Not that I didn't enjoy meeting your friends. They're great, and they obviously care a great deal about you." He turns me around and searches my eyes. "It did go well last night, right? They didn't text you to drop the loser or anything?"

Cupping his face in my hands, I reply, "Of course not." I show him the string of texts I received after they left. It's a series of thumbs-ups, clapping, and a "You go girl" from Lucinda.

He chuckles and kisses me. "Whew. I was starting to sweat. So you want to take the boat out? Or there are still a couple of paddleboards in the boathouse."

I shove his hard abs lightly. "Very funny."

Laughing, he wraps his arms around me. "That memory is one of the highlights of my life. Makes me smile every damn time I think of it."

I roll my eyes and loop my arms around his neck. "Good to know my humiliation still amuses you after all these years."

"Humiliation? Mon, you were epic! I still tell the story of how you legit walked on water."

I laugh and drop my head to his chest. I'm not sure three or four steps before I plunged into the lake could be considered walking on water.

"You got up on that paddleboard easier than any of us. Wasn't your fault the wind swept up and carried the board into the weeds before you could correct it. Damn, I still remember staring at your ass in that white bathing suit you wore."

I lift my head and gape at him. *How does he remember what I was wearing from so long ago?*

He winks at me. "Why do you think it's still one of my favorite memories?"

"I figured it was because of my reaction when the snake curled up the paddle, and I decided running on a paddleboard would somehow save me."

He hugs me closer as he laughs so hard his chest shakes beneath my cheek. "God, the paddleboard went flying behind you. We never did find the paddle you threw, even though the things float."

"That damn snake probably ate it."

"It couldn't have been more than a couple of feet long. It could not have managed it."

I shiver. "Don't remind me. In my head, it was an anaconda trying to swallow me whole." I kiss his jaw. His stubble makes my lips tingle. "Did I ever properly thank you for being my hero that day?" My terror overrode all other sensations, but I do remember Brody wading in and carrying me out of the water. It was probably the first time I realized he was no longer a little kid.

"Not the way I would've liked."

"You were sixteen."

"Your point?" His hands sculpt my sides. "You could give me a proper reward now. I figure with added interest for all the years, we probably need to spend the whole day in bed instead of going out after all."

But then the doorbell rings and wipes the grin off his face. "I'll get rid of whoever that is, and we can go back to negotiations."

"Oh, is that what we're doing?"

"Absolutely." He gives me a swift kiss and walks out of the kitchen and down the hall to the front door.

I trail behind him.

A woman stands on the front porch in shorts, a baggy T-shirt, and sandals. The way she's staring at Brody and the way he's not saying a word makes me look a little closer. Her blond hair is short, and she isn't wearing any makeup. She's probably in her late thirties or early forties and is attractive. *An old flame?* Jealousy flares, but I extinguish it quickly. I'm bound to run into women Brody has been with. I need to get used to it, or it will drive me insane. Besides, he's with me now, and that's all that matters.

"I got your email." She stuffs her hands into the back pockets of her shorts.

My eyes widen as recognition hits. *His aunt Aislinn—Linny.*

She looks past him at me standing in the hallway. "I can see you're not alone. I can come back."

Shaking his head, Brody steps back. "No, come in." His gaze meets mine over her head as she walks in. He seems shell-shocked.

"Hi. I'm Monica." I hold out my hand to her as she stands halfway down the hallway between Brody and me.

She stares at my hand for a second before shaking it. "Linny."

Excitement surges through me at the confirmation. *Linny from the journal is standing in front of me.*

Her gaze narrows. "You're the sister."

I tilt my head. "Sister?" *Does she think I'm somehow Brody's sister?*

"The sister of the boy Brody hung out with every summer."

"Oh yes. Brian." *How did she know that? Has she kept tabs on Brody?*

I glance down the hall. Brody still stands in front of the front door with his hands in his front pockets.

"Would you like something to drink?" I point behind me toward the kitchen. Then I realize she probably knows exactly where the kitchen is—she spent at least one summer here when Brody was a kid, and according to her journal, she was here during her affair with Brody's father.

Linny stares at me then looks back at Brody. "So, you know. Which one told you?"

"Neither, if you mean my parents." He glances at me. "Monica's friend found your journal buried on her property."

Shock takes over Linny's features. "I completely forgot about that journal." She turns back to me. "Your friend buy that old estate, or did they break it up into a bunch of lots and build ugly houses on them?"

"She bought the estate. Well, her husband did—before he became her husband. Franny fell in love with the estate when she was a kid, and Mitch bought it for her." *Shut up.* She doesn't need to know all that or care about it.

Linny nods, and her gaze darts down the hallway and back to me.

I search her features for similarities to Brody. It's there in the mouth and the way they both stand on the balls of their feet like they're ready to run at any moment.

*Okay, then.* Neither one of them is going to make the first move. "Why don't we go into the living room or maybe out on the deck. It's a beautiful day." *At least I hope it is.* I haven't stepped foot outside today.

"You his girlfriend or just a friend?"

Before I can answer, Brody snaps out, "Girlfriend."

*Did she ask because she wants to know why I'm taking the lead while Brody is silent by the front door, or is she only curious about his life? Does she not realize how hard this is for Brody?* She has to know what his parents are like from her own experience with them and from that summer she spent here.

I scoot past her and slip my arm through Brody's and around his back. Tension makes his muscles rigid. I rub his back. Maybe I should suggest we reschedule. He didn't have any time to prepare with her just showing up.

Brody relaxes slightly under my hand. "Is it true?"

"The journal?" She shrugs and purses her lips. "Don't remember everything I wrote about. I suspect it's as true as a teenager could be with her thoughts and feelings. I never intended for anyone to read it, though, so I didn't filter anything out."

"I think what Brody wants to know is if he's the baby you had."

"Thought we already established that." She blows out a long breath. "This is a lot harder than I thought it would be." Rubbing her hands on her hips, she turns to face us fully. "I'm sure you have a lot of questions, and I'm here to answer them as truthfully as I can."

Brody sighs. "Monica's right. Let's go in the living room."

Linny turns and walks down the hallway and to the left with no hesitation. She's standing by the window when we walk in. "Looks different. Better. No rock-hard, prissy furniture to sit on or portraits of dead people lining the walls."

I study the room, which has two sectional couches in the middle, facing each other. They're plush and covered in pillows. Definitely not rock-hard or prissy.

"Redecorated." Brody leads me over to the couch and pulls me down next to him so we're touching hip to hip, then he puts his arm around my shoulders and pulls me into his side.

Linny turns away from the window and sits across from us on the other couch. "How are your parents?"

"Same."

She nods. "Still assholes, huh?"

"Then why did you leave him with them?"

Brody freezes, and I feel his gaze.

Linny tilts her head right and left and exhales. "You read the journal, so I'm sure you know the highlights. I was sixteen and stupid, as most teenagers are. At first, I wasn't given much of a choice. At least none that I thought of at the time." She stares at Brody. "I did want you. I'm not going to lie. I was scared shitless when I found out I was pregnant. Took me some time to come to terms with it." Then Linny looks at me. "Can I take you up on that offer of a drink now?"

"Sure. What do you want?" I stand.

"Water's fine. My body is jonesing for a shot of something stronger, but I've been sober for almost fourteen years."

"Brody, anything for you?"

He shakes his head, so I walk to the kitchen. Fourteen years ago was about the time she visited that summer, according to Brody. Maybe she got sober then came here. I guzzle my own glass of water in the kitchen before returning to the living room. Neither of them looks like they've moved or spoken a word in my absence. I hand her the glass of water. As soon as I sit next to Brody, he takes my hand.

"Thanks." She drinks half of it in one gulp. "Not sure where that journal left off."

"Your parents took your baby."

Her lips tremble as she stares out the window. "I should've put up more of a fight, but they painted a very bleak future for you if I tried to keep you." She puts the glass on the table between the couches and wipes the condensation from the glass on her shorts. "I took off. Left the hospital and didn't go back. Got into a lot of bad things. Drugs. Drinking. Do you remember that summer I stayed with you here?"

Brody nods, and his fingers tighten on mine.

Her gaze returns to the window. "You were still a boy. I was six months sober then. Thought maybe I could be part of your life." Linny shrugs and continues to look out the window.

"What changed your mind?" I clasp Brody's hand in both of mine. *Barely sober, and she came back for him? Did she relapse? Or did her parents have something to do with her change of heart? Were they still alive then? They died when Brody was young, but how young?*

She scoffs. "Sassy and William managed to keep tabs on me while I was gone. They had a long list of everything I'd done wrong and threatened to tell Brody all about them. They threatened jail time, too, for some stupid shit I did when I was high, but the statute of limitations has passed on all that. They made it clear I didn't have a leg to stand on to get any type of custody of you and that I would mess up your life if I tried to be a part of it." She takes another drink of water and looks behind her. "Used to be a bar over there. Sassy poured a drink and put it in front of me. Watched while I shook and sweated through my clothes.

Then said I wasn't fit to take care of myself, let alone a kid." She turns back around and drops her gaze to the floor. "She was right."

Moments of silence pass, and I'm wishing Franny never found the journal and I never mentioned any of it to Katy or Brody.

"I'd check in on you from time to time—not so anyone would know. I figured once you were an adult, I could try again. I went to your college apartment once, but it turned out you had dropped out and left. You were hard to keep track of after that. I moved back to New Hampshire a few towns over. If you were going to come back anywhere, I figured it would be here." She glances at me. "Glad to see I was right. When I got your email, I went back and forth all night on what to say, but I couldn't think of nothing, so I got in the car and drove here."

"Why? What are you looking for?"

I squeeze Brody's thigh. He's afraid Linny is going to be like his parents and only want money from him.

"I've got my life together now. Have had a steady job for the last five years. Bought my own place. Even started dating a nice guy." Linny blows out a long breath. "I'd like a chance to get to know my son and for him to get to know me. Any chance of that happening?"

Brody is so still next to me that I'm afraid he won't answer. He's staring at Linny as if he's trying to see into her mind to determine whether he can trust her. He lets out a sigh. "There's a chance."

# Chapter Thirty

"Hi, Rosie. Sorry I haven't been here in a while." I sit on the warm grass, being careful not to crush the flowers blooming over her grave. The August sun shines down on me as I stare up at the blue sky and listen to the birds chirping to gather my thoughts.

"Franny has been acting secretive lately. I think she's going to announce she's pregnant. Lucinda is getting married next month, and instead of the big wedding you probably expect, she's having a small, intimate ceremony at her inn. Ironic that the wedding planner doesn't want a big wedding, huh? Maybe she's seen too much of the crazy planning side of weddings. Or it could be she's already had the giant wedding the first time around, and that didn't work out so well. Either way, the wedding is sure to be beautiful, and we'll all be there to celebrate with her and Bobby.

"Brody had lunch with Linny yesterday and didn't come home tense or upset. Their relationship is still a work in progress, but they're improving. They both have trust issues. The past can be hard to let go of." *Close to impossible for some.* Past hurts bring out the fear and make it hard to make choices that bring happiness rather than safety.

"Brian and Katy invited Brody and me on a double date last week. It was tense at first, but we had some good laughs. I think Brian is finally coming around. He even invited Brody to go fishing with him this week-end. Pretty sure it's not for an opportunity to drown him in the lake." *Eighty-five percent sure anyway.*

I pluck a piece of grass and spin it between my fingers. "School starts next week. Lisette quit, so she won't be there to torment me. Not sure what happened there. Tina said she was bragging about snagging a plum job at another school, but the grapevine said she was given a choice between quitting and getting fired. Guess we'll find out the truth soon enough.

"Things have been really good this summer, Rosie. I hate that I'm afraid something is going to happen to take it all away. Most of the time, I'm fine and focused on the present. But then the doubts sneak up on me. The summer is almost over, and Brody and I haven't talked about the future. I'm a small-town teacher, and he's a successful songwriter. His manager wants him to go on tour and perform instead of only concentrating on selling his songs. He writes the most beautiful music, Rosie. Is it selfish that I'm afraid of what will happen when he does?" He hasn't asked me to go with him. *And if he does?* I close my eyes and take a deep breath of the warm summer air. If he asks, I'll go with him.

"I love him, Rosie. I didn't know I could love someone so much. It's like a roller coaster of feelings all the time. I love the way he smiles at me like I'm the only woman in the world he sees. I love the way we laugh together at the silliest things. I love the way he takes care of me, doing things for me I didn't even know I wanted. My heart sings every time he walks into the room.

"He hasn't said he loves me. I'm too afraid to say it before he does. I've had to bite my tongue so many times when the words wanted to come out. I don't want to put any pressure on him to say it back—not if he doesn't feel the same. Everything is so good, but how long is he going to want me?"

"Forever, if you'll have me."

I whirl around to see Brody standing a few rows away.

He closes the distance between us and kneels next to me. "I love you, Mon. I was trying not to pressure you. It never occurred to me you were doing the same." He cups my cheek. "I've loved you for what seems like forever. I was just waiting for you to catch up."

He looks at the gravestone. "Close your eyes, Rosie. I'm going to kiss your sister now."

Laughing, I throw my arms around him as his lips meet mine.

Music blasts from my pocket. I look down and pull out my phone. "Inside Your Heaven" by Carrie Underwood plays.

"Did you change your ringtone or something?" Brody chuckles as he kisses my cheek and nuzzles my neck.

I shake my head, staring at my phone.

"Did you have your music app paused, and we bumped it on?"

Again, I shake my head. "I haven't used my music app in a couple of weeks at least." *Why would I when my boyfriend is a musician who serenades me with beautiful music?*

"Okay. Why are you staring at your phone like it's possessed?"

I look up at him with tears in my eyes.

He frowns in concern and tucks my hair behind my ear. "What is it, Mon?"

"This was Rosie's favorite song before she died. She used to hold up her hand and pretend to sing it while she danced on the bed."

He looks at her headstone then at my phone. "You think she's giving us her blessing, maybe?"

"Maybe. It's quite a coincidence, don't you think?"

Brody kisses me softly on my lips. "I think there are some things in this world we can never explain. But I do know your sister loved you, and I bet if it's at all possible, she would absolutely let you know she's watching over you and wants your happiness."

My smile wobbles as I nod, and Brody wipes the tears from my cheeks.

"I love you. I want to make you so happy you never cry again."

"Not even happy tears?"

"Is that what these are?"

"The man I love loves me back. And I feel like my sister approves. How could they not be?"

# Epilogue

Conversations fill the patio of Flannigan's Pub. All the tables are full, and several groups of people mingle on the grass outside the low fence surrounding the patio and up the hill of the park next door. This was supposed to be a private event, but word must have gotten out that Brody Jackson was playing tonight. His latest single has been climbing the charts. It surprised me when he said he was playing for the opening of Ian's new band area outside the pub.

Lucinda snuggles in Bobby's arms. The newlyweds have been rivaling Kelly and Holden for public displays of affection since they married last year. Those two sit at the table in the corner with their son, Travis, and Holden's sisters from Texas. His parents are watching the baby.

Franny rubs her pregnant belly on the other side of the table, and Mitch leans over to whisper something into her ear. She smiles and shakes her head. He's probably concerned that she came tonight since she's ready to pop at any moment.

Kerry leans close to me and holds up her bottle of beer. "Here's to the end of the school year. Another one in the bag and time to enjoy the summer."

I lift my glass of wine and clink it with her bottle. Smiling, I take a sip.

Ian walks by the table. "Ladies and gents." He tips his head in our direction as he walks onto the low stage on the end of the patio.

Rebecca slides onto the chair on the other side of Kerry with Rachelle next to her. "I've been waiting for this night since Ian told me Brody agreed to play. This is going to be awesome. Your handsome boyfriend is going to kill it." She leans over and holds up her hand for a high five.

I laugh and give her a high five. "I think he's actually a bit nervous tonight. I've never seen him get so fidgety before a performance before. He must have checked his guitar and his pockets a dozen times on the way over here." I've watched him perform in bars and larger venues, and he's never once gotten nervous. He's got his tour booked this summer and will play in arenas and stadiums. Thank goodness I have the summer off and can go with him.

Katy waves from the table next to ours, and Brian gives me a smirk. He posted a picture of me with duck lips and squinty eyes last week. I give him the evil eye. He'll get his when he's least expecting it. He has the good grace to look afraid before he grins at me.

Ian stands in front of the microphone and clears his throat. "Okay, you hooligans, quiet down if you want to get Brody Jackson out here on the stage." Conversations stop abruptly, and Ian chuckles. "Before we bring our local star out, I want to thank you for coming out to celebrate our new live music venue. A special thanks to my family and especially my beautiful wife." He blows a kiss to Rebecca while his brothers and parents hoot and holler behind me. "Love you, baby."

Rebecca cups her hands to her mouth and calls out, "Love you, too, you big lug. Now bring out Brody!"

Everyone laughs and claps.

"Come on out, Brody, before these miscreants get too drunk on the free alcohol I mistakenly agreed to."

Brody exits the side door by the stage, and we all erupt into claps and catcalls. He searches the crowd before his gaze lands on mine, and he smiles and winks. My heart skips a beat, and love fills my chest.

He adjusts the microphone and puts the strap of his guitar over his head. "Hi, folks." First, he launches into his latest hit, then he segues into the song he wrote for me, which is 'Perfection.' His eyes hold mine throughout the song.

I spot Linny on the hill behind him under a tree. Their relationship has become close, but I know she isn't a fan of the attention sitting here on the patio would bring, since a majority of the crowd read her journal and knows a lot of her life story. *Baby steps.*

Brody plays half a dozen more songs then says, "I'd like to play a new song for you before I take a break. It's a pretty special song I wrote for the love of my life. It's called 'Forever.'"

My breath locks in my lungs as he stares at me and begins to play. *He didn't play me this song. He plays all his new songs for me.*

"Forever"

*Before you, I dreamed in hours and days*
  *Never thought I'd want forever until you*
  *My past held the reins too tight*
  *And maybe I didn't care enough to fight*

*Then I saw you again*
  *My heart started beating staccato*
  *You asked how I'd been*
  *I didn't want to answer low*
  *So I gave you a wink and a grin*
  *And said, "Oh, you know me"*

*Before you, I dreamed in hours and days*
  *Never thought I'd want forever until you*
  *My past held the reins too tight*
  *And maybe I didn't care enough to fight*

. . .

*I made excuse after excuse to see you*
    *I even got a dog*
    *Suddenly, every day with you had a sky so blue*
    *And my thoughts were no longer encased in fog*


*Hope became a part of my vocabulary*
    *Love was more than a possibility*
    *Forever became my goal*


*Before you, I dreamed in hours and days*
    *Never thought I'd want forever until you*
    *My past held the reins too tight*
    *And maybe I didn't care enough to fight*
    *Girl, you made me dream*
    *You made me open my eyes*
    *You let me know I had someone on my team*
    *You helped me see through all the lies*


Brody walks off the stage as he continues to play and sing. His gaze is on mine, and my heart is in my throat. Tears spill from my eyes.


*Before you, I dreamed in hours and days*
    *Never thought I'd want forever until you*
    *My past held the reins too tight*
    *And maybe I didn't care enough to fight*


Kerry scoots her chair back, practically into the lap of Ian's brother behind us. Every gaze is on me. Cameras are pointed at us. Brody stops in front of me and drops to a knee. My lungs fill with air and freeze.

.  .  .

*Let's build our future*
    *Let's make our dreams come true*
    *I need to know*
    *Can you say yes to forever?*


Brody pulls a ring from his pocket. "Will you marry me, Monica?"

Clapping my hands over my mouth, I nod vigorously. Words have completely failed me.

Brody grins, and a roar echoes around us as everyone jumps to their feet, clapping and yelling. He hands off his guitar to Rebecca and lifts me out of my seat and into his arms. I sob into his neck.

"Just to be clear, those are happy tears, right, Mon?"

"The happiest."


Thank you reading *Heart's Melody*! If you haven't read the other Granite Cove books, you can find the links here:

*My First My Last My Only* (Franny)

*Covet thy Neighbor* (Olivia)

*No Choice at All* (Rebecca)

*Whispers & Broken Promises* (Tina)

*A Yearning Dilemma* (Kelly)

*A Change in Perspective* (Lucinda)


More Granite Cove on the Way!

Sign up for my newsletter to be the first to hear book news, get exclusive excerpts and giveaways!

# About the Author

Denise Carbo writes immersive, happily-ever-after Romance and Women's Fiction with a touch of humor and suspense. She is a voracious reader and loves to travel.

She lives in a small, picturesque, New England town with her high school sweetheart and their three amazing sons. Find out more at https://www.DeniseCarbo.com and sign up for her newsletter to be the first to her about new books, giveaways, and exclusive content. https://eepurl.com/dt5N7M

## Also by Denise Carbo

Bloodlines

**Clan. Duty. Love. Which will he choose?**

They have been here for centuries. War destroyed their planet, and now they hide among us. Malcolm Donovan, a dragon shifter, rules over one of four clans. When a clan member is murdered, he must find the killer. Nothing will disrupt his pledge to protect his clan. Nothing that is until he finds his mate.

Elsie Monroe, human to the bone, and the resort manager for the Donovan family finds herself falling in love with the charming Wyoming town, and she can't help but be drawn to the mysterious Malcolm Donovan. His rude attitude is atrocious, but his kisses can bring chocolate to a boiling point. Not to mention what he does to her body and heart.

Soon Elsie is dragged into a world of secrecy and violence. Creatures she thought were fantasy are actually real. And she is left wondering if love will be enough to capture and tame her own personal dragon.

Guilt & Redemption

Allison is a widow with dark secrets. Nightmares plague her nights. Guilt and shame shadow her days. Her new neighbor sparks feelings she thought shriveled and dead.

Jim's temporary lifestyle of renovating a house, selling it, and moving on doesn't leave room for relationships—and that's just the way he likes it. His new neighbor is not his type, but he's drawn to her anyway.

Allison's past won't stay buried. Trust is a precious commodity. Revenge, truth, and justice all have two sides. Will Allison and Jim find themselves on opposing sides?

Legacy of Magic

**An undiscovered witch and a match made in heaven or hell...**

Divorced, jobless, and homeless, Cory accepts an offer from her great aunt to begin anew. The offer comes with surprising consequences.

While solving a mysterious family secret, she is pursued by a charming lawyer and her exasperating neighbor who thinks arguing is a form of foreplay. But those circumstances are the least of her problems.

Cory soon discovers she is a witch and must learn to control her new-found powers. An ally, a confidant, and a surprise supporter guide her, but she is almost out of time. An immortal evil wants her powers and will stop at nothing to obtain them. When the battle lines are drawn, Cory must choose who is friend and who is enemy. Will love save her or endanger her even more?